An Encounter Too Far

DRAKE MEES

Acknowledgements

Special thanks are due to Linda for her valuable work on translation to and from German.

Thank you to Ludo for giving advice on the licensing of pharmaceutical products, to Elliot and Maia providing information on learning to ski, and Jenny for some proofreading.

I am grateful to all those who made comments on my first book, 'Encounters', and for the many suggestions about what should be included in the sequel. It has not been possible to include everything, but I hope you will find some of the suggestions you have made.

Finally thank you to all those who have encouraged me in the writing of this second book.

CONTENTS

1. Visit   7

2. Previously   25

3. Metz   43

4. Delving into the Past   57

5. After the War   71

6. Brian   81

7. Ambassador   101

8. Memories of Emma   115

9. Cornwall   129

10. Cologne   145

11. Turmoil   157

12. Scotland   169

13. Grindelwald   181

14. Bond, James Bond   197

15. Lost   213

16. Home   227

17. Final Assignment   243

1

Visit

It was now over a year since David and Anna had been together. They hadn't visited the UK as often as they would have liked, but now they were travelling to Penshurst for the New Year. David had sent an email to his daughter, Sue, and son, Steve, 'Anna and I would like to come over sometime after Christmas, to spend a few days with the family and meet up with old friends. We can bring presents for the children and they can have a second Christmas on one of our first nights there! Can the cottage be made ready for all of us to stay in?' David continued, 'I suggest we go to the Chafford Arms one night and then do a party at the cottage on New Year's Eve.' He was looking forward to taking Anna back home and introducing her to his friends. He did realise the visit wouldn't be without its problems for him and for

Anna. He had been aware of the slurs that circulated when Emma passed away.

'He didn't waste any time jumping into bed with a German girl after his wife died!'

'It wasn't long after the funeral that he took himself off to Germany and moved in with another woman.'

'Talk about a fast worker! It was only a matter of weeks after his wife's death that he went to live in Germany with a younger woman.'

David knew his mates hadn't involved themselves in the titillating gossip. He felt sure they would be pleased to meet his new partner and would give her a warm welcome.   However, he didn't want her to be treated like a superstar, with people queuing up to meet her. Then there were Emma's close friends. Over the years he had got to know some of them very well. He liked them and they liked him. He would find it difficult to meet them and for most it would be the first time they had spoken to him since the funeral. He knew he couldn't look them in the eye and pretend nothing had happened. They all knew their best friend had died and David seemed to show no remorse. On the contrary, he seemed to be rubbing salt in an open wound by going off and getting himself hitched to a fräulein he had met in dubious circumstances.

Sue responded positively to her father's suggestions on behalf of herself and her brother. She added, 'I notice you want us to prepare the cottage and you just fly in when all the work is done! Only joking! Steve says he will pick you up from Gatwick and looks forward to you sending flight details. Sue x.'

Steve was in the arrivals area in plenty of time to greet his father and Anna. Flight EZY8524 was shown as 'Expected', which meant he had plenty of time for a coffee and a bit of browsing. When they arrived, Anna moved forward to give him a hug and a kiss on both cheeks. Steve and David hadn't indulged in emotional greetings for many years, since Steve was a child. On this occasion he rested his hand on his father's shoulder, as he enquired about the flight. David was happy to continue pushing the trolley saying, 'I can manage this. We're travelling as light as we can.' Steve pointed out directions as he guided them to the car.

The day was cloudy and cold and the traffic moderate. He needed to keep his concentration, especially on the narrow roads as he approached Penshurst. He had never been a great conversationalist when he was driving, but on this occasion he did manage a staccato dialogue with his father who was in the front passenger seat.

'It seems ages since we've seen you. So how's the job going?'

'Fine, fine,' David said. 'Some weeks ago I was on a fact-finding trip to a distillery in Scotland.'

'Sounds interesting,' said Steve. The pause which followed indicated to Steve that his father wasn't going to say any more about this, so he changed the subject.

'So what's Stuttgart like?'

'It's a wonderful city. It has so much variety and there's a lot happening. We had hoped you would come and see us last summer.'

'That had to be knocked on the head when Jo's mother was taken ill,' Steve interrupted; wanting to clarify their absence was not due to lack of interest. 'We'll try to make it in 2016.'

When they arrived at the cottage David was the first out and opened the rear door to help Anna out. She was eager to meet members of the family, some of whom she had met before. She hugged and kissed each one. When she came to the children, Rachel, James and Fiona, Anna got on her knees, before putting her arms around them and giving each one a kiss.

Sue and Jo had put together a wonderful meal, accompanied by some excellent wine, with fruit juice or water for the children. David realised that conversation would be difficult, with so many awkward topics concerning Anna. He began by asking about things that had happened in Penshurst since he had been away, forgetting that neither of his children now lived there! This did open up further conversations about the family in particular. Anna was sitting between Steve and Jo and asked them where they lived, how they met and the work each of them did. By the end of the meal the room was buzzing and David had a contented smile on his face.

When they had finished eating and the table had been cleared, David brought in a number of small presents wrapped in brightly coloured paper and put them in front of his grandchildren. Most of them were from Grandpa and Grandma Anna, with a few from Mummy and Daddy. Sue had made a sponge to serve as a Christmas cake and had topped it with candles and edible decorations. Her father lit the candles and everyone joined in singing 'We wish you a Merry Christmas' as best they could. Rachel, James and Fiona had great fun opening their presents and playing with dolls, cars and having books read to them.

In bed that night Anna asked, 'How did that go? Did I pass?'

'It took time for people to start talking, but once they did, it really went well,' he said.

'The children are lovely and they were on their best behaviour!' Anna observed.

'They had been warned and they heeded the warning. There were obviously things we had to avoid talking about. They know very little about you, apart from the fact that you come from Germany. I'm sure they were itching to ask all sorts of questions, but they held themselves back, observing the one mouth, two ears rule.'

'What is that rule?' asked Anna.

'We have one mouth and two ears, so we should listen twice as much as we speak!' Anna laughed. 'It will be interesting to see how things go when we visit the pub for a drink and when we have a party here with lots of Emma's friends.'

Next morning David picked up the loan car Steve had booked for him. David had known Graham, the proprietor, for a good number of years.

'Good morning, Mr Burrows. I've not seen you for a long time.'

'I now live and work in Germany,' David said.

'I never knew that!'

'I moved there over a year ago, soon after my wife died.'

'Your wife died? What Mrs Burrows at the Health Centre?'

'Yes.'

'I suppose I wouldn't notice as I don't go there very often. You wait till I tell my wife!'

'I've moved in with a charming young lady and we live in Stuttgart. We're back here to celebrate the New Year with family and friends. We flew over, hence the reason I need a car.'

'Let me show you what I've got for you,' Graham said, picking up the keys. 'There we are. Fiesta Titanium. Good medium-sized motor in white. Not as large as your Mondeo. Your son said you only needed it for local trips' He opened the driver's door and showed David inside. 'Conventional 5-speed box. You'll get a nice comfortable drive. The controls are similar to your Mondeo. Do you think that will do?'

'I'm sure it will,' he said, as he followed Graham back to the office.

'Are you still driving your Mondeo?'

'No! I promised myself a German car when I went to live over there.'

'So what have you got?'

'A Merc!'

'Nice car, eh?'

'Very nice!'

'The paperwork is all ready. All you need to do is sign in the places I've indicated. Everything has to be done in triplicate these days! That's it, so away you go.'

After shaking David's hand, Graham stood there dumbfounded over the news of Emma's death.

The pub night was a great success. David had spread word to some of his mates that he would be in the Chafford Arms on Tuesday night. The response was overwhelming, whether to meet with David again, or cast an eye over his new lady friend. The landlord gave David his first pint and lots more were offered by friends, but most were declined. Some of David's mates were keen to talk about what it's like to work in Germany; how salaries compare with the UK, and what housing is like. George, one of his drinking mates, said,

'I reckon you've done yourself proud to get a good-looking young lady like that.'

Trev asked David, 'Can she speak English?'

'Of course, as well as you and I. Probably better than you!' he said with a chuckle. 'She also speaks French, Italian, and Spanish, as well as German.'

Trev was keen to continue asking questions. 'Is it alright if I go and speak to her? I mean, would she mind and would you mind?'

'That's fine, but be careful what you ask. I don't want Anna to get a bad impression of England from you lot!'

A number of David's mates did engage Anna in conversation. They told him later that she was perfectly charming and easy to talk with. A lot of ice had been broken.

A few of Emma's friends had come along with their husbands. There were apologies that they wouldn't be able to come along on New Year's Eve. David managed to have brief chats with them during the evening. He exchanged hugs and kisses with the ladies and handshakes with the men as they left. He told them he appreciated them being there and deep down inside he felt this was a start to re-building relationships that had been put under strain since the time Emma died.

The next day David thought it would be good for each part of the family to do their own thing. The others agreed. 'I would like to show Anna some of the south coast, maybe Pevensey Bay and Beachy Head.' They set off almost immediately, leaving the rest to sort themselves out.

'It's always good to get out over Christmas,' David said. 'It's so easy to eat and drink and stay indoors, when we should be having some fresh air and exercise. It's too nice to be inside.'

'I couldn't agree more,' said Anna. 'You know how much I like exercise. I'm looking forward to today.'

'I'm a bit surprised there is so much traffic when so many people are on holiday,' he said.

'Perhaps it's because there are so many on holiday. They are free to do as they wish. They can go out to see friends, or like us, they're going to do some exercise.'

'This is not a bad little car I've hired, but not a patch on my Merc!'

'Nothing is a patch on your Merc according to you!'

Once they had arrived in Pevensey, David parked the car and picked up the leaflets he had put on the rear seat.

'I thought I would read bits from some of these,' he said. 'It saves me having to remember what to tell you and probably getting it wrong. I hope that's OK with you.'

'Even if it isn't, I'm sure you will do it anyway! I can't believe I heard you say you would get something wrong. That doesn't sound like you!'

Unperturbed by Anna's remarks, David started to read, 'The Romans were the first to invade the area around Pevensey and they built a fort to ward off the Saxons.

'When the Romans left, the Saxons captured the area, but left the fort derelict and abandoned.

'Centuries later William of Normandy landed and turned the fort into Pevensey Castle by building on the Roman walls.

'During World War Two the castle became a lookout over the channel for German invaders from the sea and the air.

'Unfortunately the castle isn't open at this time of the year. We can walk through the village and down to Pevensey Bay.'

They walked on the shingle without a care in the world. Sometimes they held hands. At other times they wrapped their arms around each other. They were enjoying being alone together in the bracing sea air. Free, yet at one with each other. Occasionally they would stop for a passionate kiss.

'This is what I've missed over the past two days,' said Anna. 'We never know who might be watching at the cottage!' At that, David squeezed her closer to him and kissed her even harder.

'I'll just read the last information from my sheet. In 18th and 19th centuries this whole area was involved in smuggling. This declined after a violent clash between smugglers and customs men in 1833. During 19th century a number of Martello Towers were built along this coast, as protection against Napoleonic attack.'

Anna said, 'It seems to me the English are preoccupied with defending themselves from being attacked, either by the French or the Germans.'

'That's because we're an island nation. The last time we were invaded and conquered was by William of Normandy in 1066.'

'The other thing I would like to ask is what was being smuggled on these beaches?'

'Luxury goods and alcohol, to avoid paying taxes.'

'What are we going to do now?'

'I thought we could get something to eat in a pub and wash it down with beer or wine,' he said. 'Then I thought we could have a look at Herstmonceux village before driving home.'

The cottage was warm and cosy when people arrived for the party. Christmas decorations adorned the downstairs rooms and a large nativity had been assembled by Rachel and James with help from their father. It was supposed to be a relaxed occasion, but friends arrived looking anxious. David did his best by pouring them drinks and regaling them with stories from the past. Those who had known Steve and Sue over the years soon engaged them in conversation to catch up on news of their families. David struggled to know whether he should introduce Anna to the guests, but he thought this could make matters worse. As it was, Anna sat in isolation at one end of the room.

Steve came up with an idea. He put on a CD he thought people would dance to. David went and took Anna's hand and they jigged around the room. Then he introduced her to one of the men and he danced with one of Emma's friends. Sue danced with Tom and Steve with Jo; then they split up to dance with some of the guests. It wasn't long before everyone was dancing and the sound of laughter filled the room. The atmosphere had been transformed. It was a masterstroke from Steve that made all the difference and people responded. As David danced with different ladies he told them how much he appreciated them being there and managed a quick kiss with each of them.

Earlier in the day Anna had sent David out with a list of items she needed for the party. She warned him, 'Don't come back until you have bought everything on the list!' She spent much of the day making Eintopf, Black Forest Cake and Apple Strudel, for which she needed the ingredients. She also asked him to buy a large Stollen and a box of fireworks.

David thought this was the best time to introduce Anna to the guests, but she was now in the kitchen with Sue and Jo, putting the finishing touches to the food. Anna swept into the lounge with a large steaming pan of Eintopf. 'I thought it would be good to have a few German dishes, so I have made Eintopf, which contains meat, vegetables and broth,' she said, as she placed the pan on the table with a flourish. 'There is also Black Forest Cake, Apple Strudel, and David bought some Stollen this morning.'

Jo and Sue brought in plates piled high with other delicacies, but without the introduction afforded to Anna. Lots of guests gathered around Anna to thank her for the food and engage her in further conversation. Things turned out better than David could have wished for.

Shortly before midnight David went outside, dressed in wellies, fisherman's waterproof, thick gloves and wearing goggles. A few hardy guests went with him, but most opted to watch the fireworks from within the house. It was a good, varied display that brought a few 'Oh's' and 'Ah's' from an appreciative audience. Some of the local canine population raised strong objections.

Once David had come indoors and changed, he joined the others in the lounge. They sipped champagne and wished each other a Happy New Year.

When Steve judged the time was right, he asked people to put down their glasses and join together in singing auld lang syne. This marked the end of what had turned out to be a most successful party.

The next day the children were the only ones to stir before 9 o'clock. The morning was spent clearing up and loading and unloading the dishwasher. Later Sue and Steve looked for an opportunity to speak with their father. The chance eventually came around midnight, after everybody else had gone to bed.

'It really has been a good few days,' said David. 'I'm so pleased it's gone well. Thank you for all your hard work in making it so successful.'

Steve felt he must warn about too much self-congratulation. 'In the midst of all the good things we've enjoyed, Sue and I have to express our concern over the amount of attention you lavish on Anna.' David looked puzzled.

'You're like a little lap-dog, following her around,' Sue said.

'I admit Anna and I are devoted to each other, but is it wrong for us to show affection to each other?' he asked.

'It's not just affection. You're acting like a love-struck teenager,' Steve replied. 'Everywhere she goes you go. You're making a fool of yourself!'

David realised he had to meet this criticism head on. There might be other motives behind the words. 'Does this have anything to do with money?'

'No! Why should it?'

'I thought you may be wondering if your inheritance is safe, or whether I might include Anna in my will, so she gets a share of the estate.'

'Such an idea hasn't even entered my head,' said Steve. Sue said the same.

'I can assure you that I have no intention of changing my will. Your money is safe!'

'That's good to know!' Sue replied with a smirk on her face. 'The fact of the matter is that Steve and I are not used to you being touchy-feely with someone of the opposite sex. We can never remember you and Mum being like that.'

'Your Mum was different. She didn't express her feelings in the same way that Anna does. She was a more private person. At times it was hard to get her to show any affection. I know. I was married to her for twenty-eight years! On occasions she wouldn't even hold hands. Anna is so different. She wants us to have our arms around each other, so we can feel close.'

Steve knew this had been an uncomfortable conversation. He spoke to try and repair any holes that had opened up in their relationships, 'Perhaps we've over-stated our case. I know my thoughts were with Mum's friends in particular. I cringed inwardly as I watched you dancing with Anna in a provocative way. The occasional kiss didn't go unnoticed. It was galling for them to see their late friend's husband giving such attention to someone else.'

'OK, it was thoughtless of me to behave in the way I did at last night's party, bearing in mind the people who were there. It seemed to me by the end of the night attitudes had changed. Most of the ladies had spoken to Anna and then kissed her as they left. I'll have to moderate my affection when I'm here and particularly when your Mum's friends are around. When I'm back in Germany though, you don't know what I get up to!'

Sue sat in silence as she remembered saying similar words to her Dad about student life in London ten years earlier.

The looks on their faces indicated that the final words in this discussion had been spoken. They all stood and Steve and Sue moved to put their arms around David and Sue kissed him on the cheek. War was over, but they all knew the wounds that had been inflicted would take time to heal.

When David entered the bedroom, Anna was still awake. 'I don't know what it is' she said, 'but I can't get off to sleep. My mind is in a whirl. Who have you been talking with all this time?'

'Sue and Steve. We've been reminiscing about things in the past and thinking about the present.'

'And was lots of the conversation about your late wife?'

'Yes, we did talk about Emma.'

'And did you also talk about me? You must remember you're now with me. You can't live in the past. Your future depends on me!'

David got into bed and turned out the light. He lay there thinking about what Anna had just said. As he turned this over in his mind, he could hear her snoring gently. Only she knew what she meant!

2

Previously

David and Anna's relationship grew from the very first day. They had a care and concern for each other, wanting to support and encourage one another as best they knew how. Making love was a very special experience, as they felt the contours of their bodies locked together.

David adored Anna. She was attractive, gentle and kind. She was intelligent, witty and fun to be with. He felt extremely fortunate to have met her, albeit through a car accident. Anna thought the world of David. She admired his confident manner and the way he was concerned about every aspect of her life. Their times of intimacy were very passionate, as they indulged themselves in each other for mutual satisfaction. On one occasion David said, 'This is the point in the film when the hero lights a cigarette and lays back to enjoy the satisfaction.'

'You can do that in real life,' Anna said, 'without the need to smoke!'

David was rather envious of Anna, for the way she had slipped effortlessly into her job in the bank in Stuttgart. She hardly spoke about her work, but she was always happy and smiling when he arrived back at the flat. David, on the other hand, was finding it tough working for the Mustermann Corporation. He continued to keep the accounts, but increasingly he was being asked to provide forecasts for the performance of all those companies which came under the Mustermann umbrella.

On one occasion when he arrived for work at the castle, Klaus and Franz had been at work for some time and they were now studying spreadsheets on a monitor. They hardly shifted their gaze to acknowledge his arrival. 'Guten Morgen,' they said in unison. They then got back to the spreadsheets on the screen and the papers scattered across their desks. David hardly had time to take off his coat and sit down before Franz spoke on behalf of his father.

'We want you to examine all the records to date for the businesses in which the Mustermann Corporation has an involvement. We need to know how they will perform in the current financial year. If the predictions are unfavourable, we must encourage them to improve. If after a certain period of time, their results are still below what we require, we must cut them loose. There is no room for lame ducks. There is still a recession going on and not everyone will survive.'

David mumbled something about seeing what he could do. He wondered what had triggered this onslaught. Soon after he had taken on the post of Director of Finance, Franz spoke to him concerning the change in manufactured products from the plants the Corporation owned. Chemicals for industry would continue to be made, but there would be a radical shift to produce pesticides and pharmaceuticals. Anna told him this decision had been made while she was still employed by the Mustermanns.

'Another matter we want you to give attention to is this,' said Franz. 'You have been working here for a number of weeks and you speak only a few words of German. This is unacceptable! We are a German company, mainly doing business with German clients and you cannot understand a word they are saying and you cannot say a word in reply. This must change! There are courses online, or there is a place a few steps from your flat where you can go two nights a week. Do you understand what I am saying?'

'Yes,' said David, nodding his head. His mind went back some forty years when a teacher stood over him and said that he would only improve if he worked harder, to which he had reluctantly agreed. 'I will enrol in a suitable course when I return to the flat this evening,' he said.

As Anna prepared the meal, David set the table and poured the drinks. He needed to tell her about the discussions at the castle earlier in the day, although he realised they reflected badly on him.

'You knew this was going to happen,' Anna commented. 'At your interview Klaus made it clear that he wanted the finances of the Mustermann Corporation to be raised to new heights. This was the opportunity that presented itself to him with my departure. He is only bringing in the changes he had spoken about.'

'I realise that, but it will be my responsibility to implement these changes. I am the one who will have to decide on the businesses to be put in the firing line and I bet I will be the one pulling the trigger when it comes to the execution!'

'When I heard this being spoken about at your interview, I was annoyed,' she said. 'It seemed to imply I hadn't been doing a good job. As I thought more about this, I realised this was a good move. Taking on a new employee gave them the opportunity to draw up a new job description. As I typed up the details, I was pleased it wouldn't be me who would be doing the job. I'm sorry I won't be able to help you, because this was never part of my job description!'

'There was something else they commented on,' said David. 'They are unhappy that I speak so little German.'

'That's what I've been telling you!'

'Franz suggested an online course or evening classes.'

'After we've finished our meal, I'll go online and book up a course for you.' David reluctantly agreed with Anna's plan and settled for evening classes on Mondays and Wednesdays.

David enjoyed being with Anna and bedtime was always special for both of them. It was sometimes the only time they had to talk over what had happened during the day. Then they often indulged themselves in sex. On one occasion David raised the matter of having unprotected sex, something that had been troubling him for some time.

'We haven't used any contraception since we've been living together. The chances are that sooner or later you could become pregnant! Would you be happy with that?'

'Having thought I would never be a mother, the chance to have your child would be wonderful. What about you?'

'Perhaps I'm not as enthusiastic as you, being ten years older. It would be nice to bring up a child that we'd created, but I think I'm too old to start another family. I'll be over sixty-five before the child is fifteen.'

Anna sought to reassure David. 'You're still young and active and you have a youthful attitude to life. I don't think you behave like someone with one foot in the grave!'

He smiled. 'The trouble is it's over the next few years that age will start to catch up on me. Bits don't work as they should and start to drop off!'

'You're worrying your head over nothing. I'm not going to get pregnant. In the meantime, let's enjoy ourselves,' Anna said, pulling David on top of her. 'We can worry about the future when it comes.'

'I don't fully share your optimism, but I'm up for making the most of the here and now!'

That night David had a dream for the first time since he had been living with Anna. Everything seemed black and grey and shrouded in mist as he walked among rocks. It reminded him of the Sherlock Holmes film 'The Hound of the Baskervilles' starring Peter Cushing. He had found that quite scary when he was a teenager. His dream was less threatening, in spite of the ghostly figures that appeared from the mist, only to disappear into it again. When he awoke he could still remember the dream, but showed no sign of distress.

'We need to go away for a weekend, so you can learn to ski before all the snow disappears,' Anna said.

'It's you that thinks I need to ski! My sports were rugby and golf. I have never tried skiing in my life.'

'Then it's time you had a go. When you live in Germany you speak German. When you live in a place surrounded by snow-clad mountains, you learn to ski!'

Anna booked up a short course of lessons for David, with an instructor who came highly recommended by Franz. David was not his confident self during these early lessons. Golf was the only sport he had taken part in over the past six months and this new sport was completely different. He found it difficult to maintain concentration, learning how to stand correctly, move forward and stop. He was using muscles he had rarely used for several years and the pain began to tell. However, by the end of the course he felt better prepared to go skiing at one of the nearby resorts.

Anna hired a chalet for a weekend without telling David. She told him about it over supper a couple of nights beforehand. 'On Friday I'm suggesting we get back to the flat as soon as we can. I have a little surprise for you. We're going away for the weekend.'

'I'm working from home that day, so that's no problem for me. What have you been planning in that sweet little head of yours?'

'We're going away to a ski resort, staying in a chalet for the weekend. Then you can put into practice what you've learned from skiing lessons! The snow is good, so it should be fun.'

'It may be fun for you, but I'm not sure it will be for me!'

Anna picked up her glass and thrust it towards David. 'Here's to a wonderful weekend for both of us.' David responded somewhat tamely, picking up his glass and hardly making it chink against hers.

Anna was in charge. 'I suggest you unload the car while I prepare something to eat. I don't think I will want much at this time of night.'

'At least it will be nice to be away from Stuttgart for a few days,' he said as they finished their meal. 'The problem is I'm not really looking forward to skiing!'

'You'll be alright. It's just doing what you've learned, but on bigger slopes.'

'That's what I'm concerned about. Will I remember everything I've been taught and in particular how to stop?'

'Of course you will. I'll be there to help you. You'll be fine. And by the way, if you're intending to have sex, it had better be tonight!'

'Why?' he asked.

'Because tomorrow night and Sunday night your muscles will be so sore and every part of you will ache, so you won't be capable of doing anything else other than to lie there and groan!'

'It sounds better by the minute!' David said. 'You make it sound like a Bear Grylls' extreme adventure. I wish I was back at the flat.'

The next morning the sun blazed out of a cloudless blue sky and the virgin snow looked wonderful. Anna and David joined others jostling in the queue for the chairlift. He had taken his instructor's suggestion to buy some good quality ski boots and hire the rest of the equipment. As he looked at the other skiers he thought most resembled old campaigners, their darkened faces chiselled by long exposure to the mountain weather. They chatted away noisily, recalling previous visits and looking forward to this time's feats of daring. To David none of them looked as nervous as he felt, but perhaps they had a better way of concealing it. At last they released themselves from the chairlift and made their way on to the snow.

'I'll just go for a quick ski,' said Anna, 'Then I'll come back to help you.' With that she skied off effortlessly, as David had seen skiers do in films and on television. She rejoined him some minutes later.

'That was an impressive start,' he commented.

'I need to do better than that if I'm to reach my full potential. Now it's your turn. There's a flat area over there. I'll go first. Watch what I do. Keep your skies parallel as you push off. Then move the rear of your skis outwards so you make a snowplough and you will come to a stop. Now you try. Then keep practising it.'

Anna then demonstrated slow turns. 'Stand upright, with your knees bent and relax. Push your right ski out to go left and then your left ski to go right. Keep trying that.'

David had a few tumbles, but felt more confident as time went by. 'Isn't it about time we had a drink?'

'There's some in the bag,' she replied. 'You're doing well, gaining in confidence all the time.'

'I see what you mean about skiing being painful. My calves, buttocks, and all the other muscles are so sore. I didn't realise how unfit I was.'

'You're not unfit. It's just that you're using muscles more intensively than you usually do. You'll feel better in a day or two!'

'I'll lie there and groan later,' David quipped.

The next day it was more of the same. As the afternoon drew on David said, 'I feel pleased with myself.'

'So you should. A few weeks ago you had never been on skies. Now look at you! We're going to ski down to the bottom chairlift, gently, taking our time and stopping if we need to.' Anna then took one last ride on the chairlift and skied down again.

'I feel good about what I've achieved,' David said. 'I think I can now call myself a skier.' Anna moved close and gave him a congratulatory kiss.

Klaus and Franz were now pushing ahead with their plans for the re-organisation of the Mustermann Corporation. They had a short list of businesses to visit for encouragement or closure. There was a long list of clients who had enquired about having closer links with the Corporation, plus others that Klaus and Franz had identified as potential targets for take-over. They didn't include David in any discussions on these matters. He continued to work through the statistics and provide information for every visit they would make.

At first Klaus and/or Franz did these visitations. Later David was included and he sat in on some difficult and harrowing discussions. At times he thought Klaus and Franz had made up their minds to close a plant long before they paid a visit. He thought they could have conveyed their decision by letter or email, but instead they chose to put executives through unnecessary suffering and degrading experiences. David considered this to be grossly unfair, but he felt helpless to do anything.

So on a bright, spring morning Klaus, Franz and David set off on the autobahn to Munich, with Franz driving. They were on their way to investigate the financial state of a company founded by Helmut Weber, after whom the Weber Wollen Waren (Weber Woollen Goods) is named. When they arrived they were welcomed by Herr Weber, who took them to his office.

David shook hands and addressed his host, 'Es freut mich sehr, Sie kennen zu lernen, Herr Weber.'

'I am very pleased to meet you, Herr Weber.'

Herr Weber replied, 'Sie sind herzlich willkommen.'

'You are most welcome.'

Klaus, overhearing this conversation, complimented David on his use of German, 'Ich freue mich, dass Sie auf Deutsch sprechen.'

'It is good to hear you speaking in German.'

The rest of the discussion was conducted in German. David got the gist of the conversation, but understood little of the fine detail. After a close scrutiny of the accounts Klaus asked Herr Weber, 'Why are the profits for the last financial year so small?'

'Things have been difficult. We have cut our profit margins, hoping to sell more goods, but nobody has been buying.'

'We gave you a loan to update your machinery,' Franz interjected. 'When will that be repaid?'

'As soon as I can manage it,' said Herr Weber.

Franz asked David, 'Is three percent profit acceptable?'

'In the present financial climate it is OK.'

Klaus and Franz then had a private discussion about what action they should take. Klaus announced, 'You have six months to improve your profit to five percent; otherwise we will withdraw our support and press for closure,'

'Please, please,' said Herr Weber. 'Give me to the end of the year and a target of four percent. The new mills should increase production. It's then a matter of selling more goods.'

'That depends on your marketing strategy. It's up to you. Five percent in six months or closure.' Herr Weber looked close to tears.

Klaus and Franz locked their papers in their brief cases and stood up. They shook hands with Herr Weber and left the building. David walked behind them as they made their way to the car. He felt sick in the pit of his stomach as he heard them laughing over what had just happened. He was very unhappy about the attitude the Mustermanns had adopted. He realised it may not be long before he would be sent out alone on a mission to destroy a failing business.

One evening when David arrived home from the castle, Anna was all dressed up ready to go out. 'To what do we owe this?' he asked.

'Today I've had a great surprise. I thought we could go out for a meal and I can tell you all about it.'

David's first thought was that Anna was pregnant. His heart was pounding in his chest and he began to feel light-headed.

'OK. I'll have a shower and put on a change of clothes and then I'll be ready.'

They held hands as they walked to the restaurant, but neither of them said a word. David's mind was turning somersaults and he kept rehearsing what he would say when Anna revealed her surprise. They ordered drinks and a main course. Once the waiter had brought the drinks, David couldn't contain himself any longer.

'Has your surprise got anything to do with a little person?' he blurted out.

'What do you mean?' she queried.

'A baby?'

'No, of course not!'

'So you're not pregnant?'

'Of course I'm not!'

Somewhere in David's head a big bubble burst and his dream of fatherhood evaporated. He was so consumed by her reply that he was no longer listening to what she went on to say.

'This morning my manager called me into his office and put a proposal to me.' That one word got his attention. 'He wants me to go to our branch in Heidelberg, to help introduce some new banking procedures to the staff.'

'What did you say?'

'My manager wants me to go to Heidelberg for a week, to help staff get acquainted with new work practices.'

'What am I going to do?' David asked plaintively.

'You will be at work with the Mustermanns or here in the flat.'

'I didn't mean that. How am I going to manage?'

'You're a grown man of fifty-one and you don't think you will be able to cope on your own? You can cook. If you're at the castle you'll get a meal there. There are plenty of restaurants in Stuttgart; we've been to several of them.'

'What I really mean is I'm going to miss you.'

'I'll miss you,' Anna said. 'But it's only for five days. Absence makes the heart grow fonder. Have you never heard that saying? I'll be back on Friday, so that night can be extra special!'

'When do you go?'

'A week on Monday. I'll go by train.'

David's face said it all. He wasn't looking forward to being on his own one little bit. Anna's news had ruined his appetite for the food that had now been placed in front of him. He had said enough and they ate their meal in silence.

Anna caught an early train to Heidelberg and David drove to work at the Mustermann castle. That evening he made do with bread, a variety of cheeses and some grapes, washed down with half a bottle of wine. After working in the flat all the next day, David was keen to get out that evening. He had a shower and put on some smarter clothes and set off for the Italian Restaurant. He enjoyed his meal, but sat alone and felt lonely. As soon as he'd finished eating he paid the bill and went back to the flat.

The next night he tried a restaurant further away from the flat, and one he'd not eaten in before. He ordered a glass of wine and a main course. He thought he might have a dessert, but he left the decision about that till later. While waiting for his food to arrive he sipped his wine and let his mind wander. He considered all the work he had done that day and then inevitably his thoughts turned to Anna. In two days time she would be back. He wasn't sure he could wait that long. Suddenly he was interrupted by an attractive young lady standing at his table and holding a glass of wine.

'*Ist dieser Platz noch frei?*'
'*Is that seat free?*'
'*Ja.*'
'*Yes.*'
'*Darf ich mich hier setzen?*'
'*May I sit here?*'
'*Bitte sehr,*'
'*Please do.*'
'*Mein Name ist Berta.*'
'*My name is Berta.*'
'*Wie ist Ihr Name?*'

'*What's yours?*'

'*David. Mein Deutsch ist nicht so gut. Sprechen Sie Englisch?*'

'*David. My German is not good. Do you speak English?*'

'*Ein wenig. Sind Sie im Urlaub?*'

'*A little. Are you on holiday?*'

'*No, I live here.*'

'*What work do you do?*'

'*I look after the money for a large business.*'

'*Are you very rich?*'

'*No. The business is. What is your work?*'

'*I give pleasure to men.*'

It was fortuitous for David that the waiter brought his meal at the same time as Berta answered and he pretended not to have heard. Then her meal arrived. She spoke to break the silence.

'I'm a hooker!'

David moved the conversation to safer ground. 'Have you always lived in Stuttgart?'

'No. I was born in Munich and went to school there.'

'I used to live in England. Last year my wife died. I met a German young lady and she is now my partner.'

'Why is she not with you tonight?' asked Berta.

'She is working in Heidelberg this week.'

Further conversation ranged over comparisons between Germany and England and the amount of work available in each country. Berta said she liked London and she was a fan of Liverpool FC. David had already decided he would forgo one of the delicious desserts. As they both ate the last few mouthfuls of their meals, he decided he must get himself out of this situation as soon as he could. He wasn't surprised by Berta's final question.

'Would you like to come back to my flat for a coffee?'

'No,' he said, raising his right hand to indicate that this chance meeting was now coming to an end. 'Let me have your bill and I will pay it with mine.'

'Thank you,' Berta said, picking up her handbag. 'It has been nice to meet you,' she said shaking hands.

'Yes, and to meet you.' He picked up the two bills and took them to the counter. As they were being processed, he watched Berta walk out into the night to ply her trade.

As David walked back to the flat he thought about what had happened. He considered he had been chivalrous, accepting her to share his table, but not being tempted to do something he might regret later. That was the first time he had been propositioned by a woman! Perhaps Anna was right after all and he did have a youthful personality that made him attractive to women. All was not lost after all!

3

Metz

David had a long face when he arrived back at the flat one evening.

'What's gone wrong today?' Anna asked.

'Nothing's gone wrong! It's just that I've got to go and investigate a bank, with a view to it joining the Mustermann Corporation. I've been told it's an independent bank founded many years ago.'

'So where is this bank?'

'In Metz.'

'That's not too bad. It's not far. By the look on your face I thought it was Hamburg or you were being sent to Siberia!' she said with a laugh. 'How will you go?'

'It would be a nice run out in the Merc, but I think I'll take the train. Then I can do some preparation on the journey. The meeting is on Friday morning next week, so I'll go on Thursday. It will give me a chance to look at the city. It's a place I've not visited before. Is it in Germany or France?'

'France, but it has changed between the two countries several times over the years.'

In the days before he went to Metz David had a number of briefing meetings with Franz.

'This little bank would be a good acquisition for us. It is a bank that has been in the Kahn family for a number of generations, hence the name Banque Kahn. The present CEO is Monsieur Albert Kahn. He is very pleasant and speaks German, French and English. We have examined the accounts for 2014/15 and these show profits have increased by more than 20% in this financial year. This is encouraging. However, something we have found difficult to discover is the exact nature and details of the assets held by the bank. We understand the bank owns several properties and we need to have full details of these. The other major asset is land. Monsieur Kahn has been very evasive about revealing the position and size of this land.'

'So you want me to find out what Monsieur Kahn has kept secret from you and your father. It sounds difficult, but I'll do my best.'

David scrutinised all the accounts and reports for the Metz bank in the days before he travelled to the city. His conclusions confirmed the verbal report given by Franz that the accounts were sound and clearly presented. The one thing missing was detailed information concerning the bank's land and building assets. It was not going to be easy to make progress on this during the course of a single visit. He downloaded material about Metz on his laptop to read on the journey. He made a mental note to visit Saint Stephen's Cathedral. Anna had said the only thing she knew about Metz was that the Cathedral had some outstanding stained glass windows.

David caught an early train from Stuttgart and avidly read about Metz on his laptop. The city with a 3,000 year history became one of the principal towns after Julius Caesar conquered Gaul. The station was once the Imperial Palace for Kaiser Wilhelm II. There is a plethora of museums, art galleries and buildings of interest. The Cathedral, nicknamed the 'Good Lord's Lantern', has the largest expanse of stained glass windows in the world. He realised he would only be able to see a few of the sights on offer.

As soon as David got off the train, he crossed the road and checked into his hotel. He had a quick bite to eat, washed down with some of the local brew. Then he was off to take a closer look at the station. The building itself was reminiscent of a church, but inside, the arrivals hall and restaurant showed they were once part of the Imperial Palace, together with rooms now used as offices for the SNCF Railway Company. He took a few photos to show Anna.

He then ambled through the Imperial District of the city, with its familiar grey stone and headed for the Cathedral, the next stop on his tour. As he entered, the light coming through the stained glass was stunning. He stood in awe for a few minutes, before embarking on a tour of the building. David thought the glass in a few of the windows was plain and subdued, whereas others were spectacular. There was no other word for it. With a few more photos in the camera for Anna's benefit, he made his way to the exit.

As David left the building his path was barred by a girl of about ten, with her hand held out begging for money. A plain headscarf held back a wave of black hair from her forehead. He pushed her hand aside and continued along the path, shaking his head as he went. His mind went into overdrive as he walked away from the Cathedral. There seemed to be no adult with her. He thought she might be from one of the Eastern European countries that had joined the EU over recent years. Their citizens had the legal right to travel into other member states of the EU. David wasn't in favour of open borders and certainly not if it meant immigrants coming in to beg. Then another thought struck him, what if she came from a country well beyond the EU? Was she a refugee from the fighting in Syria or Iraq? Maybe she had been trafficked here and was now earning money for her captors by begging and being used as a sex slave, poor kid. If that was the case, he felt great pity for her, but there was no way of knowing how she got there. He couldn't get out of his mind those haunting black eyes that pierced his comfortable existence. He walked slowly back to the hotel, with no stomach for further sightseeing.

After eating in the restaurant and having a couple of glasses of wine, David turned in early. As he lay there trying to get off to sleep, he could still see those penetrating black eyes. Sleep soon overtook him, but during the night he had that dream again. He was walking amongst rocks on a misty night, in a place that he recognised, but couldn't name. Someone had a firm grip on his right hand, but he was unable to see the identity of the person who was holding on to him.

The next morning was bright and warm as David made his way from the hotel to Banque Kahn. Monsieur Kahn was waiting for him in the lobby. He stepped forward and smiled, giving David a firm handshake.

'Bon jour, Monsieur Burrows,' he said. 'I think you would prefer to conduct our business in English.'

'It would certainly make it easier for me,' David said.

Monsieur Kahn led the way along a corridor and gained entry to a room on the left using the keypad on the door. The room reminded David of the many similar rooms in which he had conducted business for IFS, having a highly-polished table, a desk, some cabinets and a variety of chairs. He guided his guest towards an opulent upright chair upholstered in brown leather and he sat down on the other side of the desk. A strong smell of polish pervaded the air.

'I hope you have received all the briefing papers I passed on to Herr Mustermann and you have had time to study them.'

'Yes, thank you. I must compliment you on the information you have made available to us and the clarity with which it has been presented.'

There was a knock on the door and a young lady entered carrying a tray with all that was required to make tea or coffee.

'Merci, Marion,' said Monsieur Kahn as he helped David to a cup of coffee.

As David sipped his drink he considered the description of Albert Kahn being very pleasant was totally justified. He was slightly shorter than David, smart-looking and always smiling. His soft voice brought David back from his thoughts.

'Have you had a chance to visit some of the places in our great city? he asked.

'Yes some. I was particularly impressed by the railway station and the Cathedral.'

'La cathédrale Saint-Etienne est la plus magnifique! I will indicate other places of interest as we walk to lunch.'

'I would appreciate that. There is so much to see that it would be helpful to be guided by someone with local knowledge.'

David then returned the conversation to the reason he was in Metz. 'As far as we at the Mustermann Corporation are concerned, the finances of the bank are sound. We would however like more details of the assets the bank has in terms of buildings and land.'

'Let me say something about the buildings, which are in different stages of their leasing agreements. Two are in the process of being re-negotiated at the present time, so it is not possible to give an exact figure for the value of the buildings and the amount they raise from leasing each year.'

David wasn't being fooled by what Albert Kahn had said and indicated this rather forcefully. 'We would need to see the complete breakdown of this for the current financial year and not some vague ideas for this asset. And that brings me to the land assets which Banque Kahn holds.'

'Again these are variable. We are negotiating to sell off some of the land we hold and it is impossible to give an exact figure until these negotiations have been concluded.'

David made it clear he didn't want to go through the same fruitless discussions. As pleasant as Albert Kahn might be, he couldn't continue to hide facts and figures from the Mustermanns. If this bank was already part of the Corporation and was under investigation, the members of the board would be told that unless every item was set out clearly in the annual report at the end of this financial year, it would be struck off. The same would apply to this bank and it would not be invited to join the Mustermann Corporation unless it put its house in order. David just could not understand why things were being cloaked in so much secrecy.

'We will expect a clear statement of the value of land you own and the revenue from land you have sold in this year's financial report if you are to be invited to join the Mustermann Corporation.'

During the walk to the restaurant, Albert Kahn pointed out some of the buildings owned by his bank. 'That insurance company is in one of our buildings and that big fashion store. You will notice some wide boulevards and lots of squares and grass areas. Most of the ancient buildings are in yellow limestone and there are many beautiful churches. If we walk this way,' he said waving his arm, 'I can show you one of the shopping malls, which we have a financial interest in. You will see this road is one of the traffic-free roads. We are a green city. The Centre Pompidou-Metz is a fascinating building near the station and it would be worth a visit before you catch your train.'

'This is a city with so much to offer. Thank you for giving me a glimpse into its beauty,' said David.

Over lunch, David and Albert's conversation turned to their families. 'I am married to a beautiful wife called Claudine,' said Albert. 'She used to be a dancer, but now she gets involved in Arts and Music projects in the city. We have two sons. One works in IT and has no interest in banking. The other has done a number of jobs and is currently working for an insurance company. I'm hoping he might follow me into banking. And what about your family?'

David took a drink of wine and said, 'I also have two children, one girl and one boy and they are both married with families. Unfortunately my wife died last year, around the time I took a job with the Mustermann

Corporation. I met up with a German lady and we have been together for six months.'

'I'm sorry to hear that your wife died and I'm sure your family was a great source of support and encouragement while you grieved over her loss. We don't see our boys that often, but I'm sure they would rally to help if we need them.'

'We have our difficulties, but I think we are now closer than we have been in the past.'

Albert Kahn chatted to the waiter as to an old friend while he was paying the bill. He then took David on a different route back to the bank. David shook hands and thanked him for making his visit so good. He expressed the hope that the financial irregularities would be sorted out and maybe he would return to Metz again in the future.

Trains to Strasbourg and on to Stuttgart were frequent, so David did avail himself of the opportunity to visit the iconic Centre Pompidou-Metz before going to the station.

Anna was keen to hear how David got on. He gave a brief outline without specific details of his meeting with Albert Kahn. She had already said she wouldn't be able to help him as Director of Finance, because the job had changed since she was employed by the Mustermanns. Anna had also implied that you didn't know who you could trust in the world of finance, so he was going to make sure any leak of information couldn't be traced back to him. He took the conversation in another direction.

'Metz is beautiful,' he said, showing Anna the photos on his camera. 'Maybe we can fit in a visit sometime.'

'Maybe. It depends on how busy we are at work.'

'You could have been more upbeat about the only thing you told me about Metz - the stained glass windows in the Cathedral.'

'Oh?'

'Amazing, stunning, fantastic, are all descriptions you could have used. I just stood there mesmerised. I then had a strange encounter as I was leaving the Cathedral. A girl of about ten was begging for money. She wore a scarf over her black hair and she had piercing black eyes. At first I thought she was Eastern European, but then it occurred to me she could have come from Asia. Maybe she was there as a result of trafficking by unscrupulous men. I didn't know what to do, but I didn't give her any money. There was nobody else around. I thought there ought to be help available for people like her, particularly if they had got away from fighting in the Middle East.'

Anna paused before she answered. 'Last night I watched the news channels showing people in boats trying to cross the Mediterranean to reach Italy. Some of the boats were so badly made that they sank and people drowned. The lucky ones were pulled out of the water by Italian fishermen or sailors. Like you, I thought something should be done to help these poor, unfortunate people. But what can we do?'

David worked at the castle each day during the following week. A number of board meetings were scheduled and few of the members knew him, so there might be opportunity for an introduction. He also thought he might pick up little snippets of information which could be very useful. On Monday he had a meeting with Klaus and Franz, to explain what had happened during his meeting in Metz. Neither of them was surprised that the Banque Kahn assets had been the stumbling block in negotiations. Later Franz typed a curt letter to Albert Kahn, indicating that if the full details of the land and buildings assets were not included in the financial report for the current year, Banque Kahn would not be considered for inclusion in the Mustermann Corporation. Two topics discussed by board members that week were the fall in the global price of oil, which had caused Corporation profits to tumble and the decreasing revenue from pharmaceutical companies since they had been taken over by the Mustermanns.

At the end of a particularly busy week David and Anna decided to dine out on Friday night. She had left for work early each morning and arrived back late each evening. They had been no more than ships passing on a restless sea.

'Let's go out and relax,' he said. 'We've hardly seen each other, let alone having time for conversation.

You've had no reason to get dressed up, so I could appreciate your figure. We've got bogged down with work and nothing else seems to matter. After just six months it's been eat, work, sleep and no sex, like an old married couple.'

'I wouldn't know about that! When you have a task to do, you need to keep focussed. It's no good behaving like young lovers, spending lots of time gazing into each other's eyes telling the other person how much you love him or her. My work at the bank is very demanding at the moment, what with people being on holiday and the bank taking on more work. Then I have other interests to pursue.'

'Such as?' David asked, looking intently at her.

'I try to go to the gym occasionally and I practise conversational French, Italian and Spanish. It's no good letting these languages lapse. I may need to use them in the future.'

'What for? Are you thinking of applying for another job?'

'No, of course I'm not, not at the present time. But you and I don't know what's around the corner. I may need to speak a number of European languages.'

'Where will I be then?'

Anna began to laugh. 'I don't know! It's just a 'what if' scenario. What would I do if something happened to you, or you lost your job, or you decided to go back to England?'

'I don't know what I would do under these circumstances,' said David. 'I haven't given it any thought. I suppose I would return to England and get myself a job there.'

'But don't you see? You don't have to panic when the time comes. You should have enough contacts and ideas you could follow through. You should have thought out a plan and then be confident and prepared for whatever might happen. Expect the worst and you might be surprised by the best!'

'I suppose I don't like to look too far ahead. I wonder how things will be in five or ten year's time. In the meantime, let's have a coffee, walk home and have sex!'

'If you must!' Anna said.

4

Delving into the Past

David picked up the phone after two rings and heard a familiar voice.

'Hi Daddy, it's Sue. How are things?'

'Good. In fact they're very good. So how are you, Tom and the children?'

'We're OK, apart from a bit of a cold. Tom and I have been talking. Before we go any further, we thought we should put you in the picture – see what you think.'

'I'm intrigued! You didn't consult your Mum and me the first time you got pregnant, so I don't think it's that. Maybe you or Tom wants to get another job and you want my advice. Or perhaps you're thinking of moving house and you need some cash. No, I don't think it's any of these. I give up. You'll have to tell me.'

'We've been talking over trying to find out something about Mum's past. We haven't much to go on, but there must be some information out there somewhere, if only we know where to find it. We need you to give the green light to start searching. We feel sure there are websites that will help.'

'I'm more than happy for you to go ahead.'

'Even if it means we find out things that may distress you?'

'Yes! I can't believe there's going to be much in the way of scandal. See what you can find out and let me know.'

Having obtained her Dad's support, Sue rang off. She didn't think there would be a problem, but she had to get him onside. She thought back to the time after her mother had died, when they were sorting out her personal effects. They came across photos of her mother with a man that was not David. Then they found a private bank account for Emma that Sue's father knew nothing about.

Some days later David received an email from Tom. 'Hi David. We've made a start on tracing Emma's early life. It hasn't been easy. We've looked on various websites, but we haven't got very far. HM Passport Office looks promising. We're working on the assumption that Emma was adopted and her surname became Simmonds. We don't know the first names of her adoptive parents. Nor do we have any idea about her date of birth or her date of adoption. Sue said she could have found some of this information from Emma's passport, but she surrendered that soon after Emma died. She has downloaded a form to obtain birth and adoption certificates, but can you help fill in any of the gaps? Look forward to hearing from you, Tom.'

David rang back immediately. 'I can help with the date of birth. Emma and I made copies of our passports. They'll be in the bureau or bedside cabinets in the main bedroom at the cottage,' he said. 'You and Sue can go over and find the information you need from Emma's passport.'

'I don't think we will do that,' said Tom. 'We'll leave you to do that the next time you are in the UK.'

'But you'll probably need that information to complete the form.'

'Sue was going to do the form, pretending she was Emma. Section 2 asks for the original birth details – surname and forenames, birth mother and father and county of birth. We know that's Yorkshire. The form then states that if the adoption took place before 12 November 1975, which it did, you must attend a meeting with an approved adoption advisor. Towards the end of the form Sue will have to sign to say she is the adopted person. Hand on heart she can't do that, especially if completion of the form flags up the fact that Emma Simmonds has died recently. In the Guidance Notes there is an email address and phone number to contact the office to discuss obtaining a birth certificate before adoption.'

'That's it!' said David. 'You need Emma's passport details from home. Then you email or phone the office and ask how you get the birth certificate.'

'OK! We'll go over to the cottage and collect the details we need. Then we can ring the office and take it from there.'

'And let me know what happens. I'm intending to bring Anna to the UK in a few weeks time.'

Sue and Tom then began to make good progress with their searches. They received confirmation that an original birth certificate for Emma was in existence. Email contact with Sheffield Archives indicated that the family could view this certificate. Elizabeth Hills from Sheffield Archives also made arrangements to view Emma's adoption papers, giving the names of her adoptive parents.

Tom and Sue set off early and picked up David and Anna from Penshurst. The sky was overcast for the first part of the journey, but once they were on the M1 the sun broke through to give a pleasant summer day. Tom used the Sat Nav to find the office in Shoreham Street. They were met in reception by Elizabeth, a smart young lady wearing a dark suit and her ID badge. She led them into a small room in which she had assembled all the information the family had requested.

'Please take a seat,' she said. 'This is Emma's birth certificate. She was born on 21st May 1966, in Hallamshire Maternity Home, Chapeltown, which is part of Sheffield. Elizabeth ran her finger across the birth certificate. 'Name Emma, girl. There is no name for the father, so perhaps she was illegitimate. Her mother's name was Jane Scoggins. The birth was registered by

Jane's mother, Dorothy, who lived at 11 Steven Crescent. She registered the birth on 26th May 1966.'

'It's just like "Who do you think you are?" said David. 'We are very grateful for your help with this.'

'And there is much more to tell you,' Elizabeth said. She moved Emma's birth certificate aside to reveal copies of the census. 'We have found out from Emma's birth certificate that the Scoggins family lived at 11 Steven Crescent. So here they are in the 1951 census: father, William, aged 24, labourer; mother, Dorothy, aged 26. Jane is recorded as one year old. If we look at the 1961 census, we see they are all still living at 11 Steven Crescent. Now Jane is 11 years old.'

Elizabeth picked up the next census. 'Now in 1971, William and Dorothy are at the same address, but Jane isn't listed,' she said. 'In that year she would have been 21. She may have moved on after getting married, or to take up employment elsewhere.'

David was keen to confirm the facts that Elizabeth had presented to them. 'If my maths is correct, Jane was 16 when she gave birth to Emma, her daughter, who became my wife,' he said.

'That seems to be the case, as far as we know it,' Elizabeth said.

'Jane was just 16 years old when she had my Mum,' said Sue. 'We can't begin to imagine what it must have been like for her, poor girl. We think she had an illegitimate baby, which is taken away for adoption and we don't know what became of Jane. So what happened to Emma after that?' Sue asked.

Elizabeth explained, 'It was usual in those days for babies and their mothers to be kept in hospital for ten days after the birth. Sometime during those ten days Emma was adopted. I have the adoption certificate here and it reads as follows:

This is to certify that

Emma Simmonds was

formally adopted by

Diane & Thomas Simmonds

on this 27th Day of May 1966

Signed: Diane Simmonds. Date: 27th May 1966

'Wow! That's proof that your mother was adopted,' Tom said to Sue.

David interrupted him and turned to Elizabeth, 'Do you have any other information for us?'

'There are two more census records I would like you to see,' she said with a smile.

'The first is for 1971. I located where Emma's new family was living. The occupants of number 46 Lyons Street in Sheffield are given as Thomas Simmonds (37) manager steel works, Diane Simmonds (35), John Simmonds (7), Emma Simmonds (5).'

'Well I'm blowed,' said David. 'We came across John when we were sorting out Emma's things last year.'

'And we thought he was Emma's lover,' said Tom. 'It turns out he's her brother!'

'Do we know if they were actually brother and sister?' David asked.

'I haven't been able to spend time researching that,' said Elizabeth. 'Let me just finish the last census. Then I can give some suggestions for further research you might like to do. In 1981 census, Thomas (47) Diane (45) and Emma Simmonds (15) are still living at 46 Lyons Street. John has reached school-leaving age and has presumably got a job and moved away. All I can say for sure is that he wasn't living with them according to the census. In the 1991 census Lyons Street no longer exists, so the trail goes cold for following up the Simmonds family.'

'I can fill in some details of what happened to Emma later on,' David said to Sue and

Tom. 'So what other ideas are you going to suggest we follow up?' he asked Elizabeth.

'You could start by following up William and Dorothy Scoggins, but as with the Simmonds family, the trail will probably end when the houses were demolished and the area was re-developed. Jane will be more difficult to trace. She may have lived in another part of Sheffield and kept a low profile. She may have married. If so you need to find out her married name, which is something I failed to discover.

'You're going to make us work hard,' said David.

Elizabeth ignored this interruption. 'You might see if you can find out what happened to John Simmonds. And if he is Emma's sibling.

David stood up and thanked Elizabeth for her painstaking research and the way she had presented the information so clearly.

'I only wish I could have spent more time on this and then perhaps I could have found out the answers to some of the questions I have left for you.' She collected together all the papers and put them in a folder and gave them to David. He took them and gave her an appreciative handshake, as did Sue, Tom and Anna. As they exited the office, they looked for somewhere to have something to eat before travelling back south.

Over lunch they discussed what they had discovered. 'I found it fascinating as I listened to Elizabeth's explanation of Emma's background,' David said. 'She did it very well.'

'Didn't you mind hearing the various revelations about Mum's mother?' asked Sue to her father. 'The two facts that we're uncertain about are whether Emma was born out of wedlock and if she and John were siblings. They are what we need to research.'

'The facts spoke for themselves and we couldn't argue with them,' said David.

Tom said, 'For me the big revelation was that Sue's Mum had been adopted. Then it came out that Sue's grandma gave birth to Emma when she was 16!'

Anna had remained silent up to this point, listening to what everybody else had to say.

Now she broke her silence. 'Firstly I thought it was a super performance by Elizabeth. It must have taken her a long time to prepare. Then she was able to provide us with so many deductions from the census forms and certificates. It was wonderful how the whole presentation flowed. Finally she gave suggestions for homework. Well done Elizabeth!'

Sue then changed the course of the conversation. 'Until now we have looked at Mum's background and life through our own eyes, maybe selfishly. Daddy has come to realise that Mummy was probably born out of wedlock and brought up by adoptive parents. How did she get on with Thomas and Diane Simmonds? Were they loving and caring? We will probably never know. How did Mum get on with John? It's likely he is still alive. It would be great to meet him. How did Mum's birth affect the Scoggins family? Jane's parents must have been mortified when they found out she was pregnant. How did she tell them?

Turning to Sue, Tom asked, 'Was your Mum's name Scoggins before she was named Simmonds?'

'Yes, she was Emma Scoggins before she was Emma Simmonds.' Sue continued, thinking out loud. 'What about Jane? How did she feel? At least she had the guts to go home. Who was the father? Did Jane have any further contact with him? I wonder what eventually happened to Jane. Where is she, if she's still alive?' After a period of silence, Anna continued the discussion, looking at events from Jane's viewpoint. She asked, 'When she found out that she was having a baby, did she look forward with anticipation to the time when she would take care of her child? Any hope of her keeping the child and building a relationship with her was soon dashed. The baby was taken from her and adopted. How must she have felt? She must have been in a complete turmoil, poor girl. But I guess it often happened like that in those days.'

As they finished their meal, they agreed there was much to be done to discover more of Emma's secrets.

'How are you two for time?' David asked his daughter and son-in-law.

'We're OK. If we get away shortly we should be back early evening. My parents are there with Rachel and James and the bed is made up ready for them to spend the night if necessary.'

As soon as they started their journey, David began to talk about Emma in a way that Sue and Tom hadn't heard him speak before. They were intrigued as revelation followed revelation. It seemed as though he wanted to provide as much background information as Elizabeth Hills had.

'My first recollection of your Mum was at the Fresher's Ball at Manchester Uni in September 1984, I think. I was in my final year doing Business Studies. Some of my mates and their girlfriends wanted to go and I just tagged along. Two of us were without partners. There were a lot of girls sitting out on their own. I went up to your Mum and asked her for a dance. She was a bit reluctant at first, but as we started dancing she threw herself into it. After the dance we went to the bar. She'd recently arrived in Manchester to do nurse training and work in a local hospital. I remember she was on lime and lemon and I was on mild,' David said. 'She was shy and didn't want to join our group. As time went by and she continued dancing with me, she became more relaxed and comfortable with people she had never met before. At the end of the night I asked if she would come out with me again. She didn't refuse, but her response wasn't the most positive I've experienced! I helped her call a taxi and gave her a hug and a quick kiss as we parted.'

David paused for breath and to think about where the story would go from here. 'Your Mum and I had exchanged telephone numbers at the Ball, but they were on landlines - no mobiles in those days! Speaking to each other proved well nigh impossible. I shared a house with some of my mates. There was a lot of leg-pulling when I first went out with Emma, but they were pretty good at passing on messages. The nurse's hostel was altogether different, filled mainly with young ladies desperate to find a husband and always on the phone!. I could never get through. Although there was a ten minute rule about using the phone, nobody kept to it. It took us over a week to arrange to meet up! After that we planned our next dates carefully and avoided using the phone.'

David paused again. 'Tell me if I'm boring you.'

'You're not,' said Sue. 'We knew about the romance between you and Mum in outline, but we didn't know any of the details, such as exactly how you met.'

As David let the silence continue, he turned to look at Anna and found she was asleep.

'I thought she might have been interested in this,' he said, 'but it's too much after a busy day!'

'I remember early on in our relationship we went for a walk on the moors. Your Mum was happy to hold my hand or link arms. If anything, I would say she was a bit clingy. As we talked, I found out she came from Sheffield. She didn't say any more than that despite my questions. She was far happier to talk about the nursing course she had just started. Each time we parted I would give her a hug and kiss. She didn't seem to participate as much as I did.'

'You'd better spare us the intimate details,' said Sue.

'Oh, I will,' replied David with a chuckle.

'Don't you think you were being unfair?' asked Sue. Poor Mum had such a bad start in life. We don't know what her adoptive parents were like. When she met you she was probably away from home for the first time. Then she meets you, Jack the Lad, and she doesn't know how to cope!'

'It didn't take long for her to fit into the group and get to know them. Most of the lads played rugby and we had a match most Saturdays. The girlfriends usually came along to support us. I remember one match in Stockport when it rained all afternoon. We all got soaked through, but the lads were able to shower and put on dry clothes!'

Tom dropped off Anna and David at the cottage. 'It was good of Pat to have left some food for us,' he said to Anna. 'A sandwich and a cup of tea will do me fine. I'll have a beer later.'

'Sue told me I missed the details of your love life while I was asleep in the car!'

'It wasn't much. Emma and I met in Manchester in 1984; I got a job in a Manchester bank and Emma worked as a nurse. We were engaged early in 1985, and married in 1986. We had a flat in the city centre. In 1988 the bank was recruiting staff to work in London and giving a financial incentive, so I took the money and ran! Within a few months we'd moved to Penshurst.

'So you didn't talk about IFS? 'How did you get a job with IFS?'

'Someone I knew told me IFS was looking for new staff. I had never heard of IFS. He said they didn't invite applications. In those days it was all done by recommendation. I thought nobody would recommend me, so I forgot all about it. Then one day I received a letter asking me to attend the IFS building in London. I got a job as a junior member of the overseas division. Later I found out it was my manager at the bank who had recommended me. Did he do it to enhance my career, or did he want to get rid of me? I'll never know!'

'As you know the world of finance is a tricky business, where there are lots of disreputable people involved,' said Anna. 'You are experiencing some of this as you work for the Mustermann Corporation. I'm sorry to tell you, it will get worse!'

5

After The War

My name is Karl. I first met Max forty years ago when he sent me a letter inviting me to meet him. Two years previously I had heard him speak at a conference called to make plans for the rebuilding of the Federal Republic of Germany. He spoke with clarity and passion. Copies were made of his script. I still keep one with me.

'Wir haben einen Krieg verloren und unser Land ist verwüstet.'

'We have lost a war and our country has been devastated,' he said.

'Unsere Industrien sind in Trümmern und unser Volk demoralisiert.'

'Our industries are in ruins and our people are demoralised.'

'The allies have not only defeated us militarily. They are now dismantling our coal and steel industries. Things look very bleak and we could tell ourselves there is nothing we can do. But there is hope, based on three factors:

1) We live in a beautiful land full of rich resources.

2) Our people have skills as engineers, technicians and scientists.

3) As a people we have a bold spirit that will enable us to succeed.

Let us rebuild homes, schools, shops and industries, but at a faster rate than we have done so far. Let us make this country great again and give our people hope for the future.'

(Translated from German)

Although Max was one of the lesser speakers, he was given a standing ovation as he sat down. This was the man who had invited me to go and see him.

I was young when the war began. I found it difficult to understand what was going on. Why should these other countries attack Germany? It seemed so one-sided and unfair! There were stories that German armies had attacked and invaded other countries. Perhaps they were just getting their own back. Rumours circulated that Jews were being rounded up and nothing more was heard about them How? Why?

As a child I was interested in how things worked. There were few toys and I would make things out of whatever I could find. I made cars out of bits of wood and metal and I built them strong enough to survive if they crashed. I used cardboard to make planes, but they never flew very well. I decorated them like the Luftwaffe planes I had seen. When I was older, I made drawings of rockets that would take men to the moon and the stars and I invented a new fuel that would propel the rockets into space by overcoming gravity! It was no surprise that I pursued my boyhood dreams into adult life and I went on to study engineering.

During the time I had before I went to see Max, I found out what I could about him. He had inherited considerable assets from banking when he was a young man. He became interested in the aspirations of the Third Reich and used much of his wealth for the manufacture of munitions. In a separate development he had acquired a stake in a number of chemical plants where chemical weapons were produced for the war effort. Before I went to see him I kept asking myself why a man with so much wealth and influence wanted to meet me and perhaps involve me in some project. Up till the moment I met him I could find no answers, but all that was to change.

Max welcomed me into his office with a firm handshake. He thanked me for going to see him and said I had been recommended to help him expand his business interests. I didn't know what he meant by that, so I didn't say anything. He talked about the present bad times and the hope he had that the nation would be great again. I agreed with him.

He told me there were leaders who shared his vision and others waiting in the wings for their time to come. He spoke about the need for economists and bankers, scientists and engineers, to make the dream become a reality. He said the whole German population must be encouraged to meet the challenge to restore the Fatherland. It just needed a catalyst to start things off and then there would be years of prosperity ahead.

As I listened to Max, I felt as I did two years previously, when he had given his impassioned speech to the conference and we all stood and applauded, to show solidarity with his oratory. On this occasion I didn't stand, but I felt the hair on the back of my neck stand for me and I knew I was somehow to be involved in Max's plans.

Max said he had looked at my credentials and found I was a design engineer with considerable potential. He realised I was a young man with a fine brain. He said the country was desperate for people like me to design and build the equipment we needed. He said the factories where weapons and explosives were made would now be used to make machinery for agriculture and forestry, to manufacture vehicles to build roads, homes, shops and offices. He ended by saying that he wanted me to head up the engineering department that would be so vital to re-build the nation. He asked for my response.

I said it would be a privilege to take on such a position and I would work to the best of my ability. Saying this, I had no doubts about my skills as an engineer, but I was uncertain if I could motivate a large team to produce the goods in the quantity and in the time-scale that Max envisaged.

It was a great experience to be involved in such a huge project to help remove the debris of defeat from our war-ravaged nation. It was all so positive after the depression of recent years. People's attitudes had changed too. Those I worked with had a spring in their step and a smile on their faces. Max was like a dog with two tails. He was elevated by many to a god-like status. Not that there were never any problems. Success was its own worst enemy. There were times when we couldn't get enough raw materials and demand for finished products outstripped supply.

I appreciated working for Max! I say 'working for' and not 'working with'. I will come to that in a minute. This man had masterminded the transformation of the Federal Republic of Germany to become one of the world's strongest economies. However the Committee he set up to oversee the entire re-building project was made up of men who should have been in charge of their individual departments, but often this was not the case. There were frequent instances of Max over-ruling heads of department. This is why I say we were 'working for' Max and not 'with him'.

Food production increased year on year and the people of West Germany enjoyed a better standard of living than for many years. All this was made possible by the increased manufacture of fertilisers and pesticides that Max had decided to implement a few years earlier. I could only admire the work that Max and others had done, to develop the West German economy to such a degree that it outstripped the economies of many European countries, including Great Britain. Things were good and so I kept my head down and ignored Max's authoritarian attitude, which had not affected me so far. One experience was to change my mind.

On one occasion I had a series of meetings with Max about the design of a whole new range of public transport vehicles. I had produced a number of scale drawings and sketches, together with estimated costs. He seemed pleased with the work I had done and it was now a matter of awaiting his approval before we could get on and build the units. I waited for one week, two weeks and then two months. Rumours reached my ears that Max was unhappy with some of the designs, but he said nothing to me. Finally Max phoned me to say that he had chosen other designs in preference to mine. I later found out that Max himself had drawn up these other designs and discarded mine. I was very angry. I had heard stories about similar things happening to some of my colleagues. I phoned Max and made an appointment to see him. What I couldn't understand was why he had expressed satisfaction with my ideas every time we met, but suddenly he found them inadequate. He could offer no good reasons at the meeting and I could only conclude that it was his way of getting rid of me. So after more than fifteen years helping to re-build the infrastructure of West Germany, I felt I must leave it all behind.

As I thought about the various options I had, my mind turned to Great Britain, where there was a similar struggle to repair what war had destroyed. Since the War my attitude had changed. There appeared to be a greater willingness towards cooperation across Europe and perhaps I could be part of that process, as well as finding myself another job. I travelled throughout England and discovered manufacturing industries were in decline. There were many people out of work in the Midlands and North of the country and I saw many examples of factories that would have to close, unless someone invested time and injected money into them. I found a small engineering business which made parts for the motor industry and I thought this would be a worthwhile purchase. I made an offer and this was accepted. My bank in Stuttgart dealt with the finances. I sent a wire to advise about the financial transactions.

I found a suitable house near to the factory, but this would require considerable repair before I could live in it. I returned to Germany feeling rather smug, having bought an engineering business at what I considered was a bargain price. I made an appointment to see Max and I couldn't wait to tell him about my acquisition.

He was sorry to hear that I would be leaving him because he thought I had great potential, but he wouldn't stand in my way. Not that I would have let him persuade me to stay with the Mustermann Corporation; I would have left anyway, with or without his blessing. I had been damaged too much to carry on working for Max. I made plans to sell the property I owned in Germany and the profit would help to pay for the repair of my new house in Great Britain. While this was being carried out I lived as a lodger in a farm house. The farmer's wife looked after me too well.

I quickly settled into running my own engineering business and my English steadily improved. There were six manual workers and a girl called Dawn who worked in the office. The previous owner had told me it was a loyal workforce and I should try to work alongside them, rather than send down orders from above. I tried to follow his advice. I found the employees not as well motivated as those in Germany, but they were eager to learn and production increased within a matter of months. I was not aware of any objection from any of the staff about working for a foreign boss; particularly one from a country that had been the enemy during the war. Nobody spoke out against the changes I had introduced. After two months I gave all the employees a modest pay increase and this was well received.

Previously, I had lived on my own, without having to cook, clean or do the laundry. I asked Dawn to advertise for a housekeeper, who could live in the spare room in my house. Eventually I appointed someone called Jane, who had recently left school and spoke with a northern accent. She settled in well and became a friend as well as a housekeeper. I gave Jane weekends off and I encouraged her to bring friends back to the house. I said she could have the Christmas holiday off and she thanked me for this.

When Jane returned early in the New Year I noticed she had put on weight. Amidst many tears she explained it wasn't because she she'd eaten too much, but because she was pregnant and this was confirmed by the nurse. Her mum and dad spent most of the holiday telling her how terrible she was and she wouldn't be able to keep the baby. Her mother did manage to find out that I was the father. Her mum wanted her back home for Mothering Sunday, so the family could make plans for her baby. I apologised for the mess I had got Jane into and said I would give her a sum of money, to be used for the upbringing of her child. She was genuinely grateful for this. Jane continued to live in Sheffield, but I heard nothing from her.

In June of 1966 I received a card announcing the birth of Emma, sent by Diane Simmonds, 46 Lyons Street, Sheffield. With it was a note saying her and her husband had adopted Emma on 27th May 1966, signed Di Simmonds. I found it disturbing that Jane had given her baby up for adoption. I wondered whose decision that was. I wondered what had happened to Jane and where she was living. I sent off a card to Di with some money, to mark Emma's birth. Several years later I contacted my solicitor and told him to change my will, so that a percentage would go to Emma when I died. Sometime later I wrote to Jane saying I wished to provide more long-term financial support to Emma. Jane told me she was no longer looking after Emma and confirmed she had been adopted by Mr and Mrs Simmonds and she gave their address. Later I asked my solicitor to alter my will, so that a percentage of my estate would go to Emma when I died. My solicitor was instructed to keep track of Emma's whereabouts. As a result of the searches that were made at the time and during the intervening years, it was discovered that you are linked to this family, and that's what has brought you here today. I hope you have enjoyed hearing my story. I hope you also approve the financial support I have promised to Emma in my will. I have also set aside some money for you.

'Hello,' said Karl, 'It's good to see you again. I'm sorry that you've had to visit me in hospital. Sometime after we met a year ago, I began to feel quite ill. I was short of breath when I went upstairs and my head throbbed when I tied my shoe laces. I felt completely washed out. I didn't do anything about it for a while, hoping it would pass.' Karl pulled himself upright and winced as he did so. 'Eventually I went to the doctor and he sent me to the hospital for tests. A few days later the doctor asked me to go and see him again. I could tell by the look on his face it was serious. He told me I had cancer in the lungs and the blood vessels going to and from the heart were clogged up. He said the cancer could have been caused by the chemicals I used in engineering. I asked him how long and he said it was months rather than years. I'm glad I went to the trouble of including Emma in my will. The solicitor has that to sort out when I go.' Karl turned to pour himself a drink and the look on his face showed he was experiencing considerable pain, as he pushed himself up from the bed. 'I'm not very old,' he said, 'not even sixty; when you hear about people in their eighties who are still fit and active. I thought I had more life left than this! It is good of you to take time to come and see me. Did you come by train? I thought you would. Thank you for coming. I'm not sure if I will see you again, John.'

A few months later John received an official-looking letter, with Davis & Hope Solicitors, on the envelope and as a letter head. The contents of the communication were brief and to the point.

Dear Mr Simmonds,

I write to respectfully inform you that Mr Karl Schmidt passed away in hospital on Sunday 6th November 1988 at the age of 59. A private burial took place on Wednesday 16th November 1988.

Sincerely,

Donald Davis

Davis & Hope Solicitors

6

Brian

Brian Huw Thomas was born on 24th March 1958 in Cardiff. His father, Huw Thomas, was a coal miner, who played rugby and sang in a male voice choir. Muriel, his mother, left work some weeks before Brian was born, but she continued to do some part-time cleaning and took in washing and ironing to make ends meet. They lived in a terrace of two up, two down, miners' cottages. Huw and Muriel had longed for a son since the day they got married and Brian was a fulfilment of that longing.

The Second World War had been over for more than ten years, but life in South Wales remained an uphill struggle and there was still much to be done to improve living conditions. Each day Huw caught the bus to and from the colliery and when Muriel was in hospital after giving birth, he carried on with the same routine. Before the birth he was offered the chance to go to an antenatal class, but he refused on the grounds that it was women's work and had nothing to do with him! All that was to change when Brian came home.

Fortunately Muriel's mother, Gladys, lived a few streets away and would come in each day for several weeks. She and Muriel would talk non-stop and she was on hand to help with the feeding, changing and bathing. Gladys would always leave before Huw arrived home, saying she didn't want to upset their family life! On the second evening, Brian screamed and couldn't be pacified. Later, when he was fed, he brought up the complete contents of his bottle. Huw wasn't used to having a baby in the house and found it difficult to cope.

'You'll have to take him to the doctor or the hospital,' he said. 'We can't have him making that amount of noise and being so sick.'

'I know,' said Muriel. 'I will try and get to see someone tomorrow.' It turned out that Brian was a sickly child during his first year and he was given some medicine to settle his stomach, but there seemed to be no remedy for his bouts of screaming.

As Brian got older he continued to look weak and pale. When he was three his mother managed to get him into a Nursery School four mornings a week. He didn't like nursery and he didn't mix well with other children, especially the boys. They wanted to play with cars and guns and race around the room, but Brian didn't want to do that. He preferred to play with the girls and their dolls and teddies. For a while Muriel didn't say anything to his dad, because she knew he thought Brian would become the archetypal, beer-swigging rugby player.

Huw thought Muriel fussed over him too much and he should be left to take a chance more often, but Brian wasn't that sort of child.

Brian always looked anxious from the day he started Infant School, as if he expected something bad to happen at any moment and it often did. He was bullied mercilessly. For his birthday his mum bought him a school bag containing pencils and crayons. During playtime some of the boys took it off his peg, kicked it around the playground and broke up the pencils and crayons and then threw them in the bin. His father was furious.

'I'll go and give that Mr Evans a piece of my tongue. As Headmaster he's supposed to be responsible for discipline, but then behaviour like this keeps on happening. If I find out who did it, I'll teach them a lesson. They won't do it again!'

'You can't do that and take the Law into your own hands. You'll be the one to get arrested and taken to court.'

During his first year at school Brian was bullied less and less. Then someone put a dead mouse into his lunch box. When he opened it at lunchtime, he screamed at the sight of the pathetic furry creature. He cried his heart out in uncontrollable sobs and it took a lot of TLC from Mrs Smith, his teacher, to get him to stop crying. After lunch Mrs Smith spoke sternly to the class and asked anyone who knew anything about the incident to go and see her, but, of course, nobody did.

Brian liked Mrs Smith. She was the one that had shielded him from the worst of the bullying and reduced it during the course of the year. On occasions she would let him stay in at playtime and lunchtime and she would read poetry to him. This seemed to help, but it did open him up to taunts of 'teacher's pet'!

As his time at Infant School was drawing to a close, Brian started getting very anxious about moving on to Junior School. He became very reclusive towards the end of the school holiday and most nights he would cry himself to sleep. Huw and Muriel tried talking it over with him, but he would say nothing about what he was afraid of.

'You'll be alright,' said Muriel, trying to ease him through this next hurdle in his life. 'You'll be in a new class with a new teacher called Miss Jones. Your dad and I will do all we can to help you.'

It took several days and many tears before Brian settled in. On many mornings he said, 'I'm not going to school today,' and it took all Muriel's guile and persuasion to get him there. After a while he came to realise Miss Jones was also a good teacher and just as kind and caring as Mrs Smith. She liked Nature Study and would often bring in objects from her garden, or things she had found on the way to school. He became fascinated with all the living things he could find and he would stick pictures of birds and flowers in an exercise book he kept for that purpose. This hobby suited Brian, as it was something he could do on his own and it encouraged him to like school.

During his last year at Junior School, Miss Jones had a word with Muriel, offering to give Brian some coaching in English, Arithmetic and General Knowledge, to prepare him for the Scholarship examination. 'He's a bright boy, Mrs Thomas, but a little extra work will make sure he passes the examination and gets a place at the Grammar School.'

'I'll have to speak to my husband and see what he thinks.'

'Alright, we've got plenty of time, but the sooner we start the better.'

Muriel thought it sounded like a good idea for Brian to have some coaching and hopefully pass the Scholarship, but Huw had a number of doubts.

'When I see those toffee-nosed brats from the Grammar School parading around Cardiff, I think it's time they got taken down a peg and do some hard work for a change.'

'But you always said you didn't want Brian to follow you and become a miner.'

'What I want more than anything is for him to leave school and get a proper job, using his hands and not sitting behind a desk. That's not proper work.'

'But if he goes to Grammar School it means he's unlikely to end up working down a mine. He'll also have a much wider choice of jobs available when he leaves school.'

'If having some extra coaching means Brian passes the Scholarship and goes to the Grammar School and doesn't have to work down a mine like me, I'm all for him having some coaching. It's only for that reason mind.'

A few days later Muriel communicated this decision to Miss Jones. Then for about a year she would go to Brian's house for an hour a week after school. This coaching set Brian apart from the rest of the class even more, but he didn't mind. He did more work during an hour with Miss Jones than he would do in a whole day at school. Besides, over time he had developed strategies to deal with the bullying and he was becoming altogether more confident.

Only five out of Brian's class of thirty-one gained a Scholarship to the Grammar School, including Brian of course. Muriel was delighted and told all her friends. Huw was proud of what his son had achieved, but refused to show it. He did keep the promise he made Brian soon after he started the coaching sessions with Miss Jones, that if he gained a place at the Grammar School, he would buy him a new bike.

Brian was determined to pass the Scholarship and have a new bike to replace his old one. Also he didn't want to let Miss Jones down, after all the time and effort she had put in. On a Saturday morning in June 1969 Brian was called to go to the yard at the back of the house, where a bike under wraps was leaning against the back wall.

'Take the paper off, lad,' his father instructed.

Brian did as he was told, but some of the paper refused to give up its secret without a struggle. Eventually Brian managed to remove all the paper to reveal a spanking new Triumph racer. He went over and gave his father a hug.

'You deserve it,' Huw said. 'You worked hard to get a place at Grammar School and you'll need it to get there come September.'

Muriel had tears in her eyes as she remembered the pale, sickly child who went through Nursery and Infant Schools and was just about to finish at Junior School. Look at him now, she thought; smiling and more confident; the world beckoning him to new experiences. However, the next few years would be somewhat traumatic for Brian.

When Brian went to Grammar School, it was the first time in his life that he enjoyed school. Science was just amazing. It was great doing experiments, but he wasn't so keen on writing up the results. Brian liked Maths in the Junior School and his interest was fostered by an excellent teacher at the Grammar School. He wasn't so keen on English and English-based subjects and later on he found Shakespeare difficult. During the first two years at his new school something happened that had the potential to unsettle Brian. The two single-sex Grammar Schools were amalgamated with a Secondary Modern School to become a High School. All the pupils who were sorted into three schools at the age of eleven were now brought together under one roof.

This change didn't seem to adversely affect Brian any more than it affected the other pupils. One thing that was a concern for Huw and Muriel at this time was that Brian was a loner, but it didn't seem to worry him at all. When he became interested in a topic, he would give it his undivided attention and nothing else seemed to matter.

On a bright autumn Saturday when there was still plenty of heat in the sun, Brian planned to do some bird watching on Barry Island. He made himself some sandwiches and put them in his back pack together with a bottle of squash and his binoculars. There was nothing he liked more than being out in the fresh air and recording the autumn-visiting birds he'd observed.

Although he wouldn't be sitting public examinations for a few years, decisions had to be taken about what subjects he would study for 'O' level. A parents evening was arranged and letters sent to all parents about the important matter of choosing options. This started discussions, which turned into arguments, between Brian and his parents about what he wanted to do when he left school.

'What are you going to do for a job when you leave school?' asked his father.

'I don't really know, but I'm keen on Science and Maths. Perhaps I'll be a scientist and work in a lab.'

'Now listen! We're not talking about a boy from Harrow or Eton; we're talking about Brian Thomas, living in Cardiff and son of Huw Thomas, a miner. You live here and in two years time you'll leave school to get a job here. What sort of job that children in Cardiff do are you interested in?'

'I don't want to get a job in Cardiff!' As he said this he knew there would be plenty of fallout from this bombshell.

His father sat there wide-eyed and speechless. His mother immediately embarked on a recovery strategy. 'We're not expecting you to go out to work tomorrow, but you need to have something in mind that you could do in Cardiff in two years time,' she said.

Brian repeated his former assertion using different words, 'I don't want to work here!' He said no more but his statement was based on his gut feeling of the past few years since he had been to High School; he didn't feel part of Cardiff; he didn't play soccer or rugby, nor did he like sailing or swimming; he hated being the son of a miner and living in a miner's cottage; there was nothing in Cardiff to keep him here and he would leave at the first opportunity.

Huw was so surprised that he didn't know what to say, without being foul-mouthed or rude. He settled for, 'We don't have to make instant decisions, either for the parents evening or for when you leave school. There's plenty of time. We can return to this later.' However, the scowl on his face spoke volumes.

The battle lines had been drawn and Brian's parents wasted no opportunity to praise the virtues of Cardiff and give information about possible jobs in the city. These tactics served to strengthen Brian's resolve to get away as soon as possible. The parents evening was a damp squib as far as Huw and Muriel were concerned. Mr Bowen, Brian's form teacher, said, 'Brian has made a good choice of options, allowing him to go in a number of different directions after taking 'O' levels.' Subject teachers were pleased with the high standard of Brian's work and only Mrs Howells, his English teacher, said he would have to work hard to gain a grade 'C' or above.

Brian's father and mother were disappointed with the parents evening. 'It seems to me,' said Huw, 'Nearly all the teachers were working on the assumption that the children would be staying on into the Sixth Form and no ideas were given about helping children to find jobs at sixteen.'

'It went against what we are trying to do to point Brian in the direction of local employment,' Muriel said. 'We'll just have to keep going with our campaign to persuade him to think locally.'

Verbal skirmishes continued on and off while Brian worked hard at his 'O' levels. He was hardly there while his parents had a meal, so any discussion had to be arranged in advance. It was agreed they would have tea together on the following Sunday.

'What is it that makes you want to go on learning and not get a job? Huw asked.

'I enjoy it,' Brian replied.

'I must say the High School has given you a good education, much better than in our day.' Muriel nodded in agreement. 'As long as you don't think you know it all and you're better than anyone else in Cardiff.'

'I don't think that. I enjoy studying and learning new things. I would love to go to university and my teachers think I can make it.'

'But what's the point in keeping on studying when you could leave school and get a job? There are jobs around here. Not like when I left school. Who's going to pay for you to go to university?'

'I should be able to get a grant, so you and mum won't have to pay.'

'That's something I suppose. One thing I'll tell you, whatever job you get, you must do some exercise. Join a rugby club and make some friends.'

'You know me,' Brian said. 'I hated rugby when I was young. How many times, Mum, did I come home crying and covered in mud. Rugby's not for me.'

Muriel then said what was on her heart. 'We don't want you to leave home and get a job somewhere else. You've not taken your 'O' levels yet and there's another two years before you would go to university. A lot can happen in that time. Perhaps you won't get enough 'O' levels or 'A' levels, or maybe you'll fall in love, marry and settle down in Cardiff.'

'Perish the thought' was the phrase that went through Brian's mind. 'I don't even know a girl, let alone someone to marry,' he said to himself. The only female he had any feelings for was Miss Jones and she was his Junior School teacher, so that wouldn't be allowed.

Huw broke the silence by helping himself to another couple of sandwiches, while Muriel poured more tea. 'The one thing in your favour is that you've never changed your mind since that first time you told us you wanted to go to university,' Huw said. 'Be determined and confident. Keep yourself fit and don't let other people walk over you.'

Later Brian thought those final remarks of his Dad were by way of accepting that he would go to university. As long as they don't try to persuade me to go to Cardiff Uni. 'No, he said to himself. I want to get right away!'

Brian passed his 'O' levels with flying colours and went on to study Maths, Further Maths and Physics at 'A' level. His teachers predicted some good grades, sufficient for him to gain entry to a university to study Maths or Physics. One teacher who studied at King's College, London and had ongoing contacts there, suggested that Brian should make King's his first choice.

Brian enjoyed being in the sixth form. He was taught by a small number of teachers and each subject had a small number of students, some of whom were doing the same three subjects as Brian. This situation was ideal for getting him to mix with other students, while working on a seemingly impossible Maths problem, or pooling results from a Physics experiment. He even started meeting some of them socially.

As 'A' levels drew to a close, Brian concentrated on two things – working hard enough to gain the 'A' level grades he required to study Maths at King's College, London, and putting plans in place to arrange suitable accommodation. He had made contact with High

School pupils from previous years who were studying in London and those in his year who would be studying other subjects in London colleges. He had a number of options available.

Brian gained the results he required and confirmed his place with Kings and his accommodation with friends. This was what he had looked forward to for several years. His father and mother didn't say anything to him about his plans.

'If you let me know the day you're leaving, I can take you to the station,' Huw said.

As Brian packed his things, it dawned on him that he was unlikely to return to Cardiff for a very long time. His parents said very little as they helped him put things in the car. His mother thrust a £10 note into his hand.

'I hope this will help,' she said.

She remained in the car wiping back the tears while Huw carried a few bags on to the station. He turned and shook hands with his son.

'I hope you have a good trip and you get on all right in London.' With that he walked back to his car, leaving Brian with his thoughts.

As he stood there he knew he had achieved what he had been aiming for over several years – to leave home and go to university. So far so good, he thought. The first part was done. Now a train journey, then on the tube, then rendezvous with friends in London. It was going to be a completely different life, one he'd longed for and he was determined to enjoy. As the train moved away from the platform he knew there was no going back.

Early days at King's were quite a new experience for Brian and opened his mind to a whole new world and way of life. There were so many events for Freshers and most offered the enticement of free food, beer or wine. Then there were the sights of London to explore and the twice-daily crowds to negotiate on his way to or from college. He managed to team up with four others and they rented a property in the East End, just beyond the financial district of the capital.

London was a microcosm of the world, with a wide variety of ages, sizes and skin colours. Brian could be rubbing shoulders with professors, dustmen, models or cleaners at any time without realising it. He was amazed by the number studying Maths at King's compared to those in the Sixth Form at High School. For lectures the hall was quite full, whereas there were smaller numbers in tutorials and the atmosphere was more informal. Slowly Brian got into the swing of university life and study. It didn't take him long to realise there were more at King's who were cleverer than him, but in the Sixth Form he had been one of the best Mathematicians.

Brian manoeuvred his way through the first and second years of his course, while enjoying a healthy social life. He had been dating a blonde girl called Linda since the start of his second year at King's and in their third year they decided to get married. The wedding took place in a registry office, Linda wearing a brightly coloured flowery dress and Brian a plain blue shirt and grey flannels. Two student colleagues acted as witnesses, a male friend of Brian's and a female friend of Linda's. Afterwards they had a meal in a pub and drank rather too much wine and beer. They spent the rest of the day sightseeing and sleeping in Hyde Park. With a little bit of shuffling around in the student house, it was possible to arrange for Brian and Linda to share the largest room.

As Finals approached, Brian sought help from the Careers Department and all the advice seemed to be pointing him towards banking or insurance. He eventually accepted a job with a bank in Central London. Linda took a job on a Management Training Scheme with Marks and Spencer.

Brian and Linda obtained their degrees, Brian saying he could have done better if he had not enjoyed such a full social life in his third year. On leaving King's they rented a flat suitably close to where they worked. As Brian lived and worked in the world of finance, he devised various schemes to maximise his salary. There seemed no point staying with the same employer, as there was no reward for loyalty. At frequent intervals he moved from bank to bank and once into insurance. Each time he moved he negotiated the maximum perks he could for insurance and preferential interest rates on his bank accounts. Linda completed her Management Training and offered herself as a trouble-shooting manager for Marks and Spencer branches in Central London. Having made money from his various financial dealings, Brian thought it was high time he and Linda should put down a deposit on a house. So in 1996 they bought a house in rural Essex, just beyond the urban sprawl. This was the opportunity for Linda to retire before her fortieth birthday. They had no children so they had no ties.

Over the next few years Brian's commute to work became more tedious and frustrating. He was on the look-out for a job with less travel and even considered setting himself up as an Independent Financial Adviser in Chelmsford. One day he received a letter inviting him to offer for the post of General Manager of a large business called International Financial Services based in London. After a series of discussions rather than interviews, Brian was offered the job. It was years later that he found out he had been nominated for the position by a German corporation.

Brian started his job with IFS in the summer of 2004. His previous jobs had been in small premises with a limited number of staff. IFS occupied monstrous premises, which made it look like an oversized comprehensive school. He wondered how many employees worked there and if he would get to know them all.

When he entered the building Sarah in reception gave him a broad smile, saying, 'Welcome to your first day at International Financial Services, Mr Thomas.'

Now that's someone whose name I should recall, he thought to himself, remembering his previous visit.

Sarah continued, 'If you follow me I'll take you to the lounge, where you will meet Mr Richard Moss, our Chief Executive Officer. He will introduce you to various departmental managers and you will have the opportunity to speak with them as a group and then individually.'

Brian was trying to think what he could say to people who had probably worked at IFS for a number of years and he was the new kid on the block. What was the advice his father gave him all those years ago? 'Be determined and confident.' He need not have been anxious, all his meetings went well.

Over time he settled in well and the person he got on with best was David Burrows. He gave Brian a warm welcome and he wasn't afraid to tell him when he had got something wrong. He had a likeable personality and a good sense of humour. On the first day David asked Brian to go out for a lunchtime drink and they found out about each other's families. It wasn't long before David and Emma had invited Brian and Linda to an evening meal and the invitation was reciprocated a few weeks later. The two couples enjoyed each other's company and they went on a week's holiday to France together.

All this was to change in August 2014 when David and Emma were on holiday and an inspection revealed that money had gone missing from David's department.

The CEO called Brian in to discuss the strategy for sorting out the mess. He appointed Brian to be the IFS member of the enquiry team, answerable to the inspectors who would return shortly to conduct the enquiry. Richard Moss made two things clear to his General Manager: that the good name of IFS should remain as untarnished as possible, with the PR team working to achieve this; the reputation of IFS mattered far beyond the reputations of any individuals.

Brian embarked on a ruthless pursuit for the truth in this whole sorry saga. When he was interviewed, David expressed the opinion that he was being made a scapegoat. As a result David handed in his notice and took a job with a German firm of financiers.

In March of this year David received an email from one of his loyal team at IFS and with whom he had occasional contact, saying that Richard Moss, the CEO, had left IFS. Within a few weeks David received another message telling him that Brian had also left. There were various rumours doing the rounds and it was difficult to separate fact from fiction. It was uncertain if Brian and Richard had resigned or if they had been dismissed.

The final bombshell was delivered to David this summer, when it was reported that Brian had been killed in a car accident. His car spun out of control on a narrow lane in Essex. No other vehicle was involved. A newspaper cutting stated that an inquest would be held shortly. David sat there looking vacantly out of the window, trying to come to terms with what he had just read. His immediate thoughts were for poor Linda. She wasn't the strongest person even at the best of times.

Perhaps he should go and see her, but what would he say?

Sometime later David had a phone call from a former colleague at IFS. 'Hello David. I thought you would like to know that the coroner at Brian's inquest reported there was a considerable quantity of cocaine in Brian's body when he died. He had been a naughty boy, hadn't he?'

As he mulled over what had happened to Brian, David was more convinced than ever that there were forces at work to remove him from IFS in the autumn of 2014. At first he and Brian had been firm buddies, but all that changed when a case of fraud was discovered in David's department when David was conveniently on holiday. David left with the offer of a post with the Mustermann Corporation. Subsequently he discovered that IFS and the Mustermann Corporation had been working together behind the scenes. Then the CEO of IFS and Brian left the organisation under suspicious circumstances. A short time later Brian was killed in a car accident whilst he was under the influence of drugs.

David broke out in a cold sweat. He and two others had left IFS. His present employers used dubious financial practices to do business. As Director of Finance he could be implicated in the corruption that was going on. He must keep his ear to the ground, but say nothing to anyone, not to his bosses, nor even to Anna. What a tangled web he had got himself involved in.

7

Ambassador

'That's it! That's it! That's it!' David kept repeating until he woke up Anna.

'What's it?' she asked.

'I know who's holding my hand in my dream.'

'Well go on then, tell me. Who is it?'

'Emma, of course. We used to go for walks on the moors. It was out in the country. Bracing. Nobody around. We had our special places. Then the murderer confessed he'd killed two more children and the police re-opened the case. Emma held my hand as if it was in a vice. She said she felt her other hand was being pulled in the opposite direction. She was petrified. We never went to the moors again'

'It must have been so frightening. Do you feel better now you can explain the dream?' Anna asked.

'It didn't worry me as much as it did Emma,' replied David. 'I'm happy now I've solved the mystery. I don't like things I can't explain or don't understand.'

'So are you now ready to go back to sleep?'

'I think so,' he said, rolling over and turning off the light.

Hot days in spring were good indicators of a hotter summer to come. As the year wore on the increased heat and humidity in Stuttgart sapped David's energy. Many times he longed for cooler, fresher weather he was used to in England. Recently there had been a flurry of emails between Sue and her dad, concerning what they had found out about Emma when they travelled to Sheffield. She and Tom had spent a weekend with Steve and Jo, her brother and sister-in-law and they had explained all the documents Elizabeth Hills had given them. It was David's suggestion that Steve and Jo should be given the task of finding Emma's brother, John, and discovering what extra information he could add to what they already knew about Emma. Steve and Jo readily accepted the challenge.

The business world was still experiencing fluctuations in fortune. Gains on stock markets one day were offset by losses the next. Added to that, the Chinese economy that had been growing year on year suddenly began to stall. Losses on the Chinese stock market were bad news for the Mustermann Corporation, which had invested heavily there and was now losing money. In addition, acquisition of some pharmaceutical product licences were not carefully examined before purchase, so some products were not as lucrative as expected. The Mustermann Corporation expanded its legal department to scrutinise licence agreements more carefully in the future.

During this time Anna was having some soul-searching moments. David's story about the girl who tried to beg money from him kept coming back to haunt her. Almost daily, television news programmes showed refugees from North Africa taking a chance to reach Europe in grossly overloaded, unseaworthy boats. One evening after dinner Anna and David talked about this.

'When I see scenes of people crossing the Mediterranean to Italy, the more I feel sorry for them,' Anna said.

'That's where we differ, 'cos I don't.'

'But they arrive in a terrible state and many die on the crossing. Don't you think they deserve the chance of a better life?'

'No! The word has got around that in Europe the streets are paved with gold and they want to come here and get rich quick,' argued David. 'There are people-traffickers making a fortune, filling their boats with these unfortunate souls, knowing that most of them will drown. There's loads of money to be made if you own a boat, in any state, on the beaches of Libya, Algeria, or Tunisia. They pocket the cash without another thought for the people they've pushed off from the beaches and who will soon be dead. The answer to this whole crisis is to have naval craft from European Union countries preventing these ramshackle boats from setting out.'

'I agree some are making a lot of money from people-trafficking. I agree some of the people are economic migrants, wanting to better themselves. If you were in their situation, wouldn't you want to escape to a country which is more peaceful, where you can work and get paid a fair wage, so you improve your standard of living? Many of these people are trying to escape from countries where there is no law and order. They repeatedly come under attack. Sometimes it happens several times a day. Many of their friends and family have lost their lives. There are increasing numbers coming from Syria and Iraq.' Anna argued her case succinctly. She continued, 'I feel sorry for the children. Isn't it a basic human right for every child to be educated? Some parents put their children on a boat and pay the fare and then see them disappear out to sea. They don't know if the children arrive in Europe or die on the voyage. This can't be right can it?'

'As I say, the simple solution is to stop these migrants or refugees leaving Africa. This seems obvious to me, David said'

'But the people still keep coming. Some of them are refugees from wars that have been raging for years.'

'OK. Send food and water, tents and blankets to the places in Italy where they arrive. And send teachers for their children.'

Anna took a pragmatic approach. 'I don't think you realise the numbers involved. It's not just Italy's problem, it has to be tackled by the whole of the EU. Most of the people who arrive in Italy don't want to stay there. They want to move on to other countries in Europe. The EU as an organisation will have to be involved sooner or later.'

Anna's clearly delivered arguments put David's simplistic solutions in the shade. He had to admit her ideas had shed new light on matters he hadn't thought about too deeply. Having changed his attitude to this crisis, he now had to ask some obvious questions.

'How do you think we should be involved in what is happening? Do we send a bit of money and then erase this whole scenario from our minds? Or should we involve ourselves in a practical way? What do we do today, tomorrow and the next day?'

Anna was pleased and more than a little surprised that David had changed his position after listening to her persuasive arguments. Now was not the time for platitudes. Her suggestions must stand a chance of being achieved. 'One thing we could do is make people aware that there is a crisis. We also need to let it be known in the right places that we want to be involved in some way,' she said. 'I could mention it to my manager and ask him to pass it round our bank network.'

'I don't think the Mustermanns will want to be involved. Unless something makes money they're not interested, particularly at the present time. However, I could ask them.'

'If they get massive publicity from the project, even if it means having to donate some Euros, I think they could be persuaded,' said Anna.

David and Anna cleared things from the table into the kitchen. He gave her a gentle kiss on the lips and then turned out the light. As he mulled things over in his mind, he had a strong feeling there were ways in which he and Anna could be involved.

The next time David went to work at the castle, he told Franz about the project. As he explained the possibilities, Franz had a scowl on his face and he seemed to be more interested in the game he was playing with the paper clips on his desk. If that was his level of interest, David didn't hold out much hope of the Mustermann Corporation being involved.

That evening, over a meal, Anna reported on an excellent meeting with her manager in Stuttgart. 'He was immediately interested in the ideas I shared. He said he knew a number of contacts whom he was sure would be interested in moving things forward. I was delighted with his response,' said Anna. 'We focussed our attention particularly on children in transit, including trafficking, meeting the educational needs, and finding permanent accommodation for these unfortunate people as a matter of urgency.'

David was impressed with the progress Anna had made. 'The discussions you had put mine into a lower league,' he said. 'I don't see any chance that the Mustermanns will get involved.'

'One topic we touched on during the last few minutes of our meeting was funding,' Anna said, trying to encourage David. 'There might be a role for you with your financial hat on.'

'Thanks! I have enough to do keeping the Mustermann partners on their toes and trying to make encouraging overtures to potential new clients, without having to do fundraising. That's never popular with any treasurer, from the smallest rugby club to the largest company.'

'Let's just wait and see,' Anna advised. 'This will take time to get off the ground.'

'Time is something we don't have,' David said, stirring himself. 'People are coming ashore every single day; sometimes it's two or three boats a day. I hope this project isn't going to get lost under so many layers of bureaurocracy.'

Time passed and nothing happened. Then David received an invitation to meet with Klaus and Franz the next time he came to the castle.

Franz spoke for both of them. 'We don't want to spend a lot of precious time, energy and money on this.' David nodded and Franz continued, 'We thought one way we could be involved would be to act as a donor or a sponsor for what is being proposed. In this way we would be giving much-needed finance and it would help the Mustermann Corporation to gain considerable publicity. This would be most beneficial under the current circumstances.'

I knew it, David thought, but how can the Mustermanns expect to gain anything from this?

Franz continued, 'There will be a need for a competent person to be the financial officer. Would you like us to mention your name in the right places to make sure you get the job?'

David shuffled uneasily in his chair. 'I'd rather not put myself forward at the moment,' he replied. 'I'll wait to see how things work out.' As he walked out of the office, he wondered if Klaus and Franz had contacted Anna before they invited David to see them.

'Good day?' asked Anna when David arrived home.

'Yes, with one interesting development. Before I tell you about that, let me ask you a question. Do you still have any contact with Klaus and Franz?'

'Very rarely. Why do you ask?'

'The Mustermanns would be willing to put up some money, in order to get publicity. Sound familiar?'

Anna didn't answer. 'I was then asked if I wanted them to use their influence, so I get appointed to be involved in finance for the project.'

'How very sweet of them. What did you say?'

'I said I'd rather not at present.'

'At least they were thinking of you and you've made more progress so far than me.'

Soon Anna received an email thanking her for the interest she had shown in the European Union's Saving Children campaign. This was followed a few days later by a letter giving further details, which she read with great interest.

Dear Mlle Mustermann,

Thank you for your interest in being involved in helping refugee children who arrive in Europe. As you will appreciate, we will require you to undergo some basic training for this work. We also need to carry out security and character checks.

I am inviting you to attend an Introductory Conference to be held 26-28 June 2015, at the Justus Lipsius building in Brussels.

Please return the reply slip at your earliest convenience, indicating your intention to attend the Conference. You should also supply details of two people, not related to you, from whom we can obtain references.

You should plan to arrive at 1600 local time for dinner at 1800. This will be followed by a brief Introductory Session. The Conference will close with lunch on Sunday 28 June 2015.

Anna's face lit up as she read the letter. 'That sounds exciting,' she said. 'So things are happening at last.'

David scanned the letter and handed it back to Anna. 'I think that's a bit much. I was the one who told you about the girl who was begging in Metz and what do I get? An invitation to count the money! And you get asked to attend a girly weekend in Brussels!'

'Oh come on David. At least Klaus and Franz asked if you wanted to be involved. And I'm sure there will be more men than girls at the Conference.'

Anna enjoyed her weekend away. She said very little about it to David. She thought it would make him angrier than he was already. Two more weekends were arranged in Bonn and Strasbourg.

When Anna arrived home from the training session, she took out her certificate and showed it to David. It said that 'Anna Mustermann has been appointed to be a Goodwill Ambassador for Children.' She was delighted and it showed. This was the first time for weeks that David had seen her in such high spirits.

'That's great and I'm so proud of you,' David said. Somehow he didn't feel his congratulations had registered.

David was becoming increasingly concerned about Anna. She was far from her happy-go-lucky self during the previous months. She looked tired and drawn and she hadn't really started any of her ambassadorial duties. In fact she looked more relaxed and full of joie de vivre around the times of the three training weekends. If she continued in the same state for much longer, David would have to say something.

It happened one evening when Anna almost literally staggered through the door of the flat, looking pale and exhausted.

'What's the matter,' David asked. 'You look in a terrible state.'

'I must say I feel tired,' Anna admitted.

'Sit down and I'll get you a drink. Coffee or wine?'

'I'll have a small glass of wine.'

He poured the wine and gave it to her and then sat beside her on the sofa.

'What is wrong? Your job at the bank was going so well.'

'It still is.'

'Your appointment as a Children's Ambassador gave you a new lease of life. I think it's a marvellous accolade. I should keep on telling you how well you've done and how proud I am of you.'

'I think you've told me often enough!'

'Can you try to put into words what's going on in your life, so I can try to help?'

'I don't think I can at the moment. Maybe later.'

'We've not been intimate for a while now and that's a sure indication that something's wrong.'

'I know,' said Anna, dabbing her eyes with a tissue.

'The way you look and behave affects me. Your vivacious personality was what attracted me to you. Remember those first meetings in car parks and coffee shops?' Anna attempted a smile. 'You're the reason I'm in Germany. I was besotted by you and I still love you dearly.'

Anna put on a sad face, almost, it seemed, to order. She picked up her glass and took it into the kitchen and then busied herself in preparing a meal. David did something he rarely did; he put the television on and watched the News. Anna could hear it from the kitchen and came to watch when she heard an item about refugees.

'Look at them,' said David, 'Not just from Africa, but also from Afghanistan, Syria and Iraq. They're talking about hundreds of thousands now, no longer boatloads. The largest mass migration since World War Two.'

'If you watch, you'll notice there are quite a lot of adults with children.' Anna remarked. 'We saw a clip at one of the training sessions and our attention was drawn to the number of children we could see. That means work for me. At the first weekend they were talking about a steady trickle and we might be needed for a week at a time. Now it looks like a torrent of refugees and I've been warned to be ready to be away for two or three weeks.'

'What about getting time off?'

'My manager is very good and said I can negotiate some time off when I need it. Also I'll continue to get paid by the bank as their contribution to helping the refugees.'

'That's generous. Your manager has been very good to you for the short time you've been at the bank. Something you've not said is what exactly you have to do.'

'As I understand it, I walk along with the refugees and talk to children and parents as best I can. If I come across children with health problems, or who are lacking food and water, I pass on details to other Ambassadors who have responsibility for these. I'm primarily there for education. I try to teach children to sing songs to keep their spirits up. In a way I can't wait to get started, but that will mean that things are getting worse. I met some refugees for a short time on one of the training weekends. It will be good to do it for real for a period of time.'

The television news moved on and the meal was ready. As they ate, Anna and David talked more about the refugee crisis. David noticed this helped Anna to relax and she had more colour in her cheeks. The conversation went on late into the night. Anna thought she might get a call to go and do her work with children as early as the beginning of August. David expressed the view that she must have a complete break when she returned home.

'One thing you wanted to do sometime was to go to Cornwall for a holiday,' David said. 'How about we try to book something up over the next few days, so after Mlle Ambassador has done her duty, we can go off to England and relax?'

'That sounds a great idea,' Anna said. David thought she really meant what she said.

8

Memories of Emma

'The earliest memory I have of our Emma is of a little girl wearing dresses that were too big   for her. She also cried a lot,' he said. 'She often had her hair in bunches and she wore National Health glasses.' You wouldn't say she was the prettiest girl at school. As her teeth grew, they stuck out from her mouth and this made her appearance even worse. She was never a happy child, often bumping or knocking herself or falling over. Me mum said that was how she got bruises on her arms and legs, but I wasn't so sure,' he said ruefully.

'Me and our Emma were adopted. It wasn't till later we found that out. Life at home weren't easy.' John had a serious look on his face, as if painful memories were coming back. It was a look John had more than once when he was talking with Steve and Jo. 'It was years later that we found out the people we called our mum and dad weren't our real mum and dad. Neighbours called our mum Di, short for Diane. She was lovely and kind. She didn't go out to work, but spent all her time looking after us and Tommy, our dad. He wasn't so nice. He worked in a factory. He would shout at us when we did things wrong and he would smack us if he got really angry. He used to shout at our mum sometimes. There were days when she was sad and she looked as if she'd been crying. I reckon he hit her too.'

'If life at home was difficult, at school it was worse. Our Emma didn't know what she was to do most of the time. She had no idea of letters, words or numbers. From the time she started school I can remember her having to stay in at playtime or lunchtime to finish her work. When she did go out to play, nobody wanted to play with her. When she had to line up she was often pushed out of the line. I remember once someone tripped her up and she grazed her hands and knees.'

'I was two years older than our Emma,' John said. 'I got picked on when I first went to school, but I would stick up for meself. Once I got into a fight with Danny Woods over some cards. We both got cuts on the face and eventually we stopped fighting. I think that fight made me one of the gang and nobody picked on me after that.

'I thought I had to look after our Emma at school. When I first went to school me mum would walk me to school and push our Emma in the pushchair. Then when our Emma started our mum would walk us both to school and collect us after. As we got older I was given the job of taking our Emma, as well as meself. Other children didn't pick on her so much when they knew I was her brother. They would have to face me if they did! I felt good, looking after me little sister. But she was a poor little thing as against the others in her class.' John paused for a while to get his breath. It was just as if he had turned the page of a book and now he was ready for the next part of the story.

'Me mum were really smashing. She loved us and was patient with us. Every night till we were quite old she would read us a story before bed. She would help us do colouring and painting and she'd take us out on trips. She would try to calm our dad when he got angry over something we'd done and he didn't like. She often took the blame for me and our Emma. As I got older, our mum and I would try to keep our Emma from our Dad's words and fists. Years later our Emma would thank me for doing this. As the years went by, our Emma and I realised we were getting through the storms. He didn't hit us so often and his shouting was not so loud. We were of an age when we could talk about it and work out ways to avoid our dad's punishment. We also thought he was getting wiser and figured out we might tell someone what was going on.'

At this point John stopped his narrative and stood up. 'I had better get you something to eat and drink,' he said. 'Would sandwiches and cake be alright with a cup of tea or coffee?'

'No, no!' Steve and Jo said together.

'A cup of tea and a biscuit will be fine,' said Jo.

'Are you sure? I should put on a better spread than that for my sister's child and spouse whom I've just met. I never knew you existed until a few weeks ago!'

Steve confirmed what Jo had said, 'Tea and biscuits are OK.' John accepted this and went out to make the tea. Jo and Steve spoke in whispers in the few moments they had to mull over what John had told them.

'Doesn't sound a very happy house, does it?' asked Jo.

'What's surprising to me,' said Steve, 'is the girl he was telling us about was my mum. It didn't sound a bit like her. By the time I can remember her, she was pleasant and a good mum, though neither Sue nor I dare step out of line! I can't remember her having buck teeth or glasses, though I knew she wore contacts.' His words tailed off as John returned with the teas.

'So,' said John, 'let me ask you a few questions, before I continue my story. I need to sort out how I'm related to you and other people in your family. Our Emma married David and they became mother and father to one of you.'

'Me,' said Steve.

'Because David married our Emma, that makes him my brother-in-law. I'm uncle to your father and mother's children. That makes you my nephew,' he said looking at Steve. 'I think you said you had a sister.'

'Yes, Sue. She's slightly older than me. She's married to Tom.'

'Like with you, Steve, I'm her uncle and she's my niece. Where do she and her husband live?'

'Maldon in Essex. They have two children, Rachel and James. I think you would be their great uncle. We have one daughter who's still a baby, so you're her great uncle too.'

'So whereabouts do you two live?'

'In Sussex, not far from the coast.'

'Let me return to my story,' John said. 'When we moved to secondary school I saw less of our Emma. She was in a different building for some of the time. I still thought I had to look after her though. I wasn't very good at school. I used to go fishing a lot and going on long walks to track animals and go bird watching. Me mum would pack me up some sandwiches and drink and off I'd go. I used to love it. I looked forward to the time I would leave school and get a job. Tommy kept saying nobody would employ me 'cos I wouldn't have any CSE's. In the term that I left school I spent weekends working as a volunteer for the Forestry Commission in various places in the West Riding. It was much better than being at school, even though I didn't get paid.'

'I left school in 1980 at the age of sixteen. I came to work for the Forestry Commission in North Yorkshire. At first I lived with another forestry worker and his wife. Then this small cottage was done up and I've lived here ever since. I love it, so quiet and peaceful, surrounded by trees. It's not everyone's choice.' Steve and Jo's expressions indicated it was not somewhere they would choose to live!

'When I left home, it meant our Emma was on her own and she no longer had me to help and support her. Me mum would be fine, but it was Tommy I was worried about, with his barbed tongue and flying fists. I received several letters from our Emma during the first few months after I'd left. She told me how bad things were and said she missed me terribly. I think I might have written to her once! Then the letters got less and I thought things must have settled down, but maybe she didn't have the time to write. When we met up she told me the first year was the worst and after that Tommy resorted to criticizing her lifestyle and what she hoped to do in the future. Apparently he kept on telling her she was wasting her time with her head always in books and she should go out into the real world and get herself a job. Perhaps he thought I had done the right thing, in spite of what he said at the time.'

'I don't know what persuaded her, but our Emma decided she wanted to be a nurse. She sent me a brief note to tell me. Then during her last year at school she wrote to say she had got a place in a teaching hospital in Manchester. I did reply this time to congratulate her, as I realised she too would be moving away from our home in Sheffield and the influence of Di and Tommy. At this stage of our lives we were probably closer than at any time before or since and we did meet up a few times.'

'It wasn't long after our Emma had gone to Manchester to start nurse training that I received a letter telling me all about it. She said this was what she had set her heart on doing and it was like a dream come true. I was pleased for her, after all the bad experiences she had when she was young. A few days later another letter arrived giving me an update. She continued to say how good the training course was, but there was another, more important reason, for writing. She had met this charming young man called David, who she described as lively, witty and fun to be with. As she went on to describe other things about this young man, I realised these were the qualities she had expected from a gentle, loving father that were sadly missing from Tommy's life. I also had to accept these were not things that I could have provided as her elder brother. She concluded her letter by saying she thought she was falling in love and questioning why she should be so lucky, when David had so many other girls to choose from.'

'I now had to accept that David had replaced me as Emma's friend and helper. I no longer had a part to play in her life and I now needed to distance myself from her. I wrote briefly to offer congratulations and I said I was sad she would be disappearing from my life. Early in 1985 I had a note from Emma saying that she and David were engaged. In June of that year we met up for lunch in Leeds. The last time I had seen Emma she was still at school. In those few years she had become an attractive young lady. We talked about our childhood in Sheffield and she asked me about my work. Neither of us said anything about the fact that this was probably the last time we would meet. We got a passer-by to take a photo of us and then we said goodbye, each of us with tears in our eyes. After that I had no further contact with

Emma. I now know from our phone conversation, Steve, she and David married in 1986, had two children and went to live in Penshurst. You also told me that Emma sadly died in November last year. Shall we have a short break?' asked John, wiping back a tear. 'I'll go and make some more tea.'

John continued, 'That was the end of the story as far as I was concerned, the final details being filled in by you very recently. However, in 1986 I received a mysterious letter from someone called Karl Schmidt. He said he was born in Germany and came to England after the War. He ran an engineering factory near Birmingham. He told me he was trying to trace people who were related to him. He had found out where Emma Burrows (Simmonds) was living and he understood I was related to her in some way. I was puzzled by this and wondered how I could be related to someone from Germany. I wrote and told him I was Emma's brother, but I couldn't work out how we could be related to him. He said he was keen to carry on investigating his family and said he would find out details of my parents and grandparents if I agreed. I said I was happy for him to do this. A number of letters went backwards and forwards between us over the course of a few weeks. He then invited me to visit him at his home in Warwickshire.

He made me very welcome and immediately launched into his life history. As part of this, he told me that Emma's mother gave birth to Emma and he was the father, but they weren't married.'

'So Mum had a German father and a mother who wasn't married to him,' Steve said. Turning to John he said, 'Do you know if you are Mum's real brother or brother by adoption?'

'No, I don't. Karl did say he would try to find out about this and loads of other things, but when I met him he said he had nothing new to tell me'

'That's a pity. It doesn't move us any further forward. We'll see what we can do. Sue and Dad found out a lot from somewhere in Sheffield.'

'Karl told me he had made a will promising some of what he would leave when he died to Emma. He rang me early in 1988 to tell me he had cancer. He said he would like to see me before he died. A few weeks later he rang me to say he was in hospital and gave me directions to get there. When I went to see him he was in great pain, but there was nothing I could do or say. He died soon after we met.'

'We can add a final piece of information to this particular jigsaw,' said Steve. 'When we were clearing out my Mum's possessions, we came across statements for her private bank account, which none of us knew existed. The first deposit of £36,000 was made in May 1989 and we now know where that came from.'

'Phew,' John said, making a whistling sound with his lips. 'As much as that? Karl wanted to make sure his daughter was provided for after he'd gone.'

'What we can't be sure of is whether Mum knew where it came from. The other question, to which we have no answer, is what was she intending to do with the money? We're deeply grateful, John, for all you've been able to tell us about our Emma, especially your first-hand account of what things were like when you were growing up together. I can tell you too that you've unwittingly solved another mystery. When we were searching through Emma's effects, we came across a photo of her arm-in-arm with a young man. On the back was written 1985. My Dad was livid, because it was taken after he and Mum were engaged. There was also a postcard from the Lake District sent by John. We did put two and two together and thought the man in the photo was John, but we still had ideas that there might have been a secret affair going on. John, we have now met you and can confirm that it was you and Mum in the photo. You don't look much older!' As he said this, Steve got up and gave John a big hug.

'Oh don't,' said John, 'you're getting me going again. That was the last time I saw Emma!'

Steve and Jo gave John a final hug as they left him on his doorstep.

'We've certainly got a lot to tell Dad, and Sue and Tom,' Steve said enthusiastically. 'It's just so incredible what we managed to find out. We'd spoken on the phone, but we'd never met him before. By the end it was as if we'd always known him.'

Jo added to the state of euphoria they were both feeling, 'In a way this kind of story is reserved for films and television soaps, but it's actually happened to an ordinary family, our family. What are some of the things we should pass on to the others?'

'Mum and John grew up in an alien household. That drew them close together and they supported each other. When John left home and they lived apart, it was tough for both of them.'

'But your Mum soon found your Dad as a substitute for John. Poor John was left on his own. The difficulties he experienced came to the surface towards the end of the story. He wasn't the only one in tears at the close.'

'What we must do is write up what we heard as a story,' said Steve. 'When we get home we need to put our heads together and put it on the laptop. Then we can share it with the others. We can't let this be lost. It could be the inspiration for a book one day! I suppose the thing that stands out for me is the fact that Mum's Dad was a German who came to this country after the War. We can now explain where Mum's private bank account came from. Meeting John was such an experience. What a fantastic day we've had!'

Jo went on to extol John's virtues, 'He's the one I feel sorry for. At the end, he's been left with nothing, or should I say, no-one. I think he really loved your Mum, just like lovers who fall in love and marry. For him there was no happy ending. I feel so sorry for John.'

During the next couple of days Jo and Steve wrestled with making a true account from what John had told them. They argued and quibbled over how to express what John had said as accurately as possible. By the end they expressed satisfaction over what they had produced. They couldn't wait to email it to the rest of the family.

Tom and Sue were gripped by the saga of Emma's childhood. They thought Steve and Jo had produced an excellent record of what they had been told. Their only regret was that they weren't able to be there to hear from John for themselves. They rang Jo and Steve to congratulate them.

David's response was altogether different. They thought he would be as excited as Sue and Tom, but he wasn't. He gave the document a cursory glance and then rang Steve and Jo. 'Thanks for doing that,' David said. 'I hope I will get a chance to read it sometime. Anna and I are completely consumed with one thing right now; the plight of refugees entering Europe. Anna is likely to leave any day soon, to help where she can. If you've seen the pictures on the television, you will know why. There are thousands and thousands of people making their way from Italy and Greece to northern Europe. There are increasing numbers trying to escape from the fighting in Syria and Iraq. They're walking along railway lines to reach their destinations. Some countries have closed their borders to deny access. The whole situation is volatile. We can only wonder what Anna can do to help. She's been appointed so she must go, whenever the call comes. She's likely to be away for about three weeks. Please think about her. I'll try to let you know what's happening as soon as I hear anything.'

Within a few days Anna received her orders to go. She was already packed and David went with her to the station. They enjoyed a passionate, but brief, embrace; it was as much as they could snatch under the circumstances. David ambled back to the flat and busied himself in Mustermann Corporation matters for the rest of the day. He watched television news bulletins as often as possible. His mind was in turmoil and there were so many unanswered questions. Wherever Anna ended up, how safe and secure was it? Where exactly would she be working? Where would she sleep? What food would she eat? What were the dangers of injury or death? Would he hear from her? When would she return? The more he pondered the possibilities, the more anxious he became. He was a bag of nerves. He couldn't contemplate what he would be like in three weeks time when Anna should return.

9

Cornwall

Time passed so slowly. By the end of the day on which Anna left, David had decided he must go and work at the castle each day, so he got out of the flat. Life without Anna was intolerable. He found it difficult to sleep and there was no-one to talk to.

One morning when he arrived for work, Franz invited him to step into his office. Franz commended David, 'We are grateful for what you have done so far, in identifying failing companies we own, and so provide ammunition for Klaus and me when we visit. Also, we are pleased with the recommendations you have made to draw new businesses into the Mustermann Corporation. These have been accurately assessed. This is very good. For those that are never going to make the grade, open a folder and file their details away. You will probably never have to open that folder again.'

David gained the impression that Franz was pleased with David's work over the past few months. Often Franz and Klaus paid compliments to prepare the way for some new avenue of work they were sending in his direction. His thoughts were justified.

'You will remember the problems we had with short-life licences for pharmaceutical products, which you brought to our attention. We would like you to keep this matter under close scrutiny. Hence you will keep us informed of the dates when each product will come out of license. You will also have to check the licenses of all products which have the potential for us to purchase.' When David had raised these problems in the past and they had been discussed by the board, he remembered quite clearly that it was agreed to expand the legal department, to make sure these mistakes didn't occur again.

'One last request,' said Franz, 'that you provide board members with a weekly statement of account.' David nodded and grunted his agreement. There's not much there then he thought! At least they were all areas with which he was familiar and they should pose no difficulties. They would also give him plenty to keep his mind occupied while Anna was away. He went to his monitor to look at the product licenses and he started on this straight away.

Over the next few days David watched the news avidly to see if Anna had been caught on camera. He never managed to catch even the slightest glimpse of her. One evening he went online, to check out hotels, flights and car hire for a trip to Cornwall, which they intended doing before she went away, but never managed to fit in. Anna had said she was likely to be away for two to three weeks, so he felt confident that the last week in August would be OK for their holiday. David booked a hotel near Padstow, Sunday to Sunday, return flights from Stuttgart to Bristol, and a hire car at the Airport.

Each day the television news portrayed more pictures of the escalating refugee crisis. More people were prepared to take a chance to cross the sea and increasing numbers perished on the way. There were harrowing scenes of people walking for miles, while others gave up from exhaustion. The European Union came in for lots of criticism, because there seemed to be no guidance on what to do. The governments in some countries were opening their borders to enable refugees to pass through, but others were sealing their borders. Some countries welcomed refugees with open arms, while others didn't want them at any price. As David continued to watch he realised the situation was reaching breaking point. If something wasn't done quickly, he thought, there would be a human disaster of gigantic proportions.

The day before the three weeks was up, David received a text from Anna, 'I'm on my way home. Should arr lunchtime tomoro. Time tbc. A xx.' She arrived on time according to her later text. David was there to meet her and took charge of the luggage. Anna looked pale and exhausted. Apart from David saying, 'It's lovely to have you home, darling,' as he gave her a brief kiss at the station, they walked home in silence. He knew she wouldn't want him to make a lot of fuss. Her most pressing needs were a shower, an opportunity to chill out and have a simple meal. He prepared fish salad with wine or fruit juice. He didn't want to put Anna under pressure after all she had been through, but David would like to know something about what she had been doing.

'Judging by your appearance, it was hard work while you were away,' David said.

'It wasn't so much hard as relentless.' Anna replied. 'People just kept coming hour after hour. I had to help children and this was much as I expected from what we did in training. There were just so many of them!'

'What was the food like?'

'It was OK. Nothing special, but adequate.'

'What about sleeping arrangements, toilets and showers?' he enquired.

'All the domestic arrangements were the best that could be provided under the circumstances. I have to admit I didn't sleep well. It was a strange place and there were some weird noises in the night.'

'Now you can relax and have a good sleep tonight,' David said. 'I've booked up flights to the UK and accommodation in Cornwall for next week. We fly out tomorrow at 1420. I'll give you a hand with the packing.' Anna smiled as she remembered David's previous attempts at putting clothes in a suitcase.

'I think I will be able to manage that on my own!' she said.

Next day they had a good flight from Stuttgart to Bristol. David picked up the hire car from the airport and took the M5 for most of the journey to Padstow. Anna fell asleep soon after leaving the airport and only woke up when David was negotiating the bends on the final part of the journey.

'This is fabulous,' Anna remarked as they entered the hotel and checked in at reception. Having confirmed that meals were still being served, they wasted no time in having a shower, changing their clothes and going down to the restaurant. While they were eating , they talked over what they were expecting from the holiday.

David said, 'I want to forget about work, relax and enjoy myself.'

'Much the same, I suppose. Perhaps I'll go for a swim in the hotel pool a few times,' said Anna.

'It would be good to get back to that loving relationship we enjoyed when we were first together,' he said. 'That would mean enjoying sex more often than we have at home over recent weeks.' Anna reached out and put her hand on David's shoulder.

'That would be good; I look forward to it! I'm sorry I've been so preoccupied with other matters, but there's nothing here to get in the way.'

'It's not just been you, I've been working myself to a standstill at times,' he said. 'I think I'll go and have a quick drink in the bar.'

'I won't join you; I'll go upstairs and read,' Anna said. 'I'll look forward to seeing you upstairs.'

David kept his word and had only one quick drink. He used the stairs rather than the lift and when he reached their room Anna was asleep. So it's not tonight he thought to himself!

'Sleep well last night?' David enquired as they ate their breakfast.

'Yes I did actually,' replied Anna.

'So you should. You were well away when I came to bed, not long after you!'

'I needed it. I feel fully refreshed and ready to do whatever we're going to do today.'

David thought a little explanation might be in order. 'We've not had a chance to make plans for where we want to go and what we want to do. The only possible time was on the flight here, but we both nodded off several times. I thought today we don't need anything too strenuous. I'm suggesting we might have a look at Padstow and then find Constantine Bay, which has some rave reviews. Then a bit of history to finish, as we visit Tintagel.

'Sounds OK to me,' Anna said, 'but what do I know, I've never been here before? Do I get to choose where we go on some of the other days?'

'You can do that tonight when we get back to the hotel.'

'I think Padstow is fascinating,' said Anna, looking in yet another shop window. 'It's a quaint fishing village with a lovely harbour and such a great variety of shops.'

'It must be time for coffee soon,' David said.

'It hasn't been that long since you had coffee with your breakfast,' she said.

'I'm ready for another,' David countered.

After their brief stop, they walked along the Carmel Trail, which is on an old railway track alongside the river estuary. 'There are some stunning views here,' Anna commented.

'I don't remember ever doing this walk before,' replied David. 'It really is beautiful.'

On returning to Padstow Anna and David found a suitable restaurant where they could have lunch. 'I'm ready for this,' she remarked. 'I thought today was going to have gentle activity with nothing too strenuous.'

'At least it was flat,' David replied.

'I think I coped with the walk as well as you did,' Anna said. 'It must mean I'm as fit as you.'

David ignored what Anna had said and went on to explain what he proposed doing after lunch. 'We'll drive to Constantine Bay and hopefully we can find a quiet spot to chill out.' Once again it was the kind of scene depicted on postcards that made it very popular.

They did manage to find a secluded place where they could sunbathe without too many onlookers.

'I have to agree with you, on the evidence of today, Cornwall is a beautiful place,' said Anna.

'I thought you would like it,' David said. 'Already you are looking much better. It must be the bracing sea air that has put colour back into your cheeks. See what happens when you relax. How can we set aside more time for each other when we get back home?'

Anna had a worried look on her face. 'I honestly don't know,' she said. 'When we're back in Stuttgart, you will be working on strategies to improve the Mustermann finances and I will be back working in the bank. I may have to go off and do another stint helping refugee children. Adding that all together, it really doesn't leave us with any time to relax and develop our relationship.'

'That sounds a defeatist attitude,'

'I'm just being realistic,' Anna said. 'See if you come up with any bright ideas.'

David sidestepped the challenge and changed the subject on the way back to the car. 'We're going to finish today with a visit to Tintagel. It's said that King Arthur was born in Tintagel Castle. His wife was Queen Guinevere and he ruled a kingdom called Camelot. Merlin was a magician who helped him and Lancelot was one of the Knights of the Round Table. The Knights spent a lot of their time searching for the Holy Grail. That's a quick summary. Some people say this is true, but others say it's a fairy tale. You will find out more as we walk around Tintagel and there'll be plenty of books on the subject. You'll have to make up your own mind, if Arthur really existed, or if the whole thing is a made-up story.'

'I'm intrigued,' said Anna, 'I'm looking forward to finding out more.'

As they walked across the wooden footbridge to the island, Anna suddenly caught her breath. 'I had a strange feeling as I looked at the castle ruins, that something bad is going to happen.'

'I hope not,' said David. 'It's stood here for a long time, so we should be safe for the next few minutes.'

As they wandered around the remains of the castle Anna confirmed the feeling she had experienced previously.

When they returned to Tintagel Village Anna bought a book entitled 'Arthurian Legends'. 'I don't want a great volume that I can't understand and won't read,' Anna said. 'I need a book which describes the main details of King Arthur and the people and places associated with him. I look forward to reading this.'

David led the way into King's Hall and again Anna said she had an uneasy feeling inside her. He suggested they should not stay any longer and should make their way back to the hotel.

That evening after they had eaten Anna was keen to have her say about what they might do for the rest of the week. 'I would like to spend time in the Health Spa and Pool,' she said.

'I'm sure I can find something to do while you are indulging yourself,' said David with a grin. 'The other possibilities are Land's End and a nearby beautiful, white beach, the South Coast, the Lizard Peninsula, and the Eden Project. Falmouth is also a delightful place to visit. I would like to play a round of golf sometime; perhaps I could do that when you're being pampered.'

'I thought you were asking me what I would like to do. While I was still thinking, you reel off a list of places we could visit,' objected Anna.

'Sorry! They were just suggestions I made because you are new to Cornwall,' he said. Anna quickly went back to her book and became engrossed in the story of King Arthur. David had such a thirst, but he dare not go for a drink in the bar, in case he came back and found Anna asleep again!

'That was good!' Anna said after it was over. 'Perhaps I hadn't appreciated what I'd been missing.' David put his arm round her shoulder and kissed her neck, as Anna moved her body in appreciation of his attention. She in turn dug her fingers into the skin on David's shoulders. Although this hurt, he didn't complain. To him there was no hurt in true love.

Sadly next morning the weather was overcast; with none of the heat of the previous day. 'I think we should go to the Eden Project today,' David suggested. 'Just a little sun and the Biomes get hot.' He was right and they certainly did. He had visited this research project at least once and many years ago. So much had changed he found the experience as fascinating as Anna did. Both agreed the day was a great success, in spite of the inclement weather.

After having a shower and change of clothes, they went to the bar for a much-needed drink. David also had another motive, wanting to meet someone who would join him for a round of golf. There were no other customers in the bar when he and Anna entered. Soon, however, they were joined by two men Anna guessed were older than David. Both were sporting moustaches and had unusually long hair and were wearing patterned jumpers that would have been more appropriate in the winter.

'Hello, I'm Bill,' said one of them, 'and this is Andy.' David introduced himself and Anna.

'Are you here on holiday,' Andy enquired, then assuming he knew the answer, he carried straight on with his next question, 'Whereabouts in the UK do you live?'

Anna stopped him in his tracks, 'We don't live in the UK, we live in Germany!'

Both men gave Anna and David a strange look and then Bill said, 'But you're not German, are you?'

'I am,' replied Anna.

'I'm English,' added David. At this Bill and Andy turned away and said a few words that Anna and David were unable to hear.

'So what brings you two lads to Cornwall,' enquired David.

''We're on a mission, to play as many golf courses in Devon and Cornwall as we can in two weeks.'

'We've met the right people to speak to,' David said to Anna. Then to Bill and Andy he said, 'Do you mind if I make it a three-ball one day?'

'You'll be welcome, as long as you don't slow us down! What's your handicap,' Andy asked, looking at David.

'Twenty,'

'Ok, we can accommodate you.'

'What are your handicaps?' asked David.

'Twelve and fifteen,' came the reply.

'Do I assume you have golf widows somewhere?' David asked.

'Oh yes,' said Bill.

'They're with us,' Andy added. 'They spend their time doing antiques fairs, arts exhibitions and stately homes.'

'So what did you both do in your working life,' enquired David.

'A little bit of this,' said Bill.

'And a little bit of that,' added Andy. They couldn't be persuaded to give any more details. All they added was, 'It was very profitable,' said in unison as they drained their glasses. David and Anna avoided looking at each other, as they knew they would have collapsed in laughter had they done so!

The agreement before the start of play was that the loser would have to buy the drinks. David had resigned himself to finishing in last place and he wasn't surprised that he had to pay at the bar when they finished.

Over lunch Anna told David about her experiences. Other ladies went to the same session as Anna and she guessed they were the wives of Bill and Andy. 'The strange thing was there were three of them,' said Anna.

'Perhaps this group of ladies was unrelated to Bill and Andy. Or maybe Bill and Andy's wives had a friend who always joined them. I did wonder if there was a third man, who wasn't able to come on this occasion.'

'Or perhaps he's inside!' added David. They both laughed.

'When they got ready for treatment, I was amazed at the amount of jewellery they had to take off; rings of different shapes and sizes, earrings, necklaces and bangles. They all spoke with a strong accent I recognised as coming from London. They looked about the right age to be wives of Bill and Andy. They were about the same height, short and dumpy. None of them dived into the pool. They lowered themselves in. They didn't swim, but just splashed around in the water.'

Next morning there was no sign of them. They had left the hotel.

Anna was intrigued by the signpost at Lands End, giving mileages to New York and other places. She and David scrambled around on the rocks and made the most of being out in the bracing fresh air. Afterwards they went and did some sunbathing on the stunning Porthcurno beach, famed for its white sand. It was breezier than previously, but they managed to find a sheltered spot where they could sunbathe in private. Anna continued to read about Arthur and his Knights, while David slept intermittently.

When she noticed David's eyes were open Anna asked him, 'Why does the author write about humans and animals in the same piece of text? I'm confused.'

David propped himself up on one elbow and tried to sound as though he was speaking with authority. 'This is when it's difficult to distinguish between fact and fiction, reality and fairy story,' he said.

'What you just said hasn't helped me at all!' Anna replied. 'And what's this Holy Grail the Knights are constantly searching for?'

'I think it's some sort of metal plate linked to Jesus,' David said. 'I can't give you an accurate description, because nobody in the past or present has ever found it.'

'It seems a pointless exercise to carry on looking for it,' Anna said. 'They might as well give up!'

'Ah! said David, rising to the challenge. 'It's a bit like love; you never know when you're going to stumble on it, like in a car park in Caretan!' he said with a twinkle in his eye.

For the final two days of their holiday David and Anna agreed to explore the Lizard Peninsula, and some fishing villages along the South Coast. After they had visited Lizard Point on Friday morning, David insisted that they walk to Mullion and have a look at the coves on the way. It was while they were admiring the rugged nature of the cliffs and the picturesque views that a fishing boat appeared, travelling in the same direction as they were.

'There's something flashing on that boat,' said Anna. David could see it too, but he couldn't make out what was causing it. 'Could it be somebody is trying to get a message to us?' she asked.

'You mean like smugglers used to do in the past? That sounds very unlikely. Why try to contact us? Perhaps there's someone else around here waiting for a message.'

They continued standing on the same spot, watching the light get dimmer as the boat moved further away, eventually disappearing from view. David and Anna retraced their steps and then did a walk around Cadgwith, using directions in a leaflet David had picked up from the hotel. When they arrived back they made the most of the refreshments served by the pub in Cadgwith. Their only disappointment was that they had to walk uphill to the car park.

As Anna and David set off on their final day David pointed out that the fishing villages they would visit all had things in common, yet they were unique. Again Anna soaked up the atmosphere of each place. She found the views breathtaking. She was fast running out of superlatives to describe them.

'That can't be bad!' David said, 'Coffee in Mevagissey, lunch in Truro and a cream tea in

Falmouth.' Anna put her arm around David's waist, pulling him close and he reciprocated.

'I'm really glad you brought me to Cornwall,' Anna remarked. 'I've loved every minute of it. It's not just been about visiting beautiful places; we've discovered ourselves again and found each other.'

David reminded Anna of some experiences during their trip. 'Don't forget Arthur, real King or a fairy tale character? What caused your strange feelings in Tintagel? Then there were my golf buddies and their eccentric wives or someone else's wives! Finally the fishing boat with the flashing light. How significant are any or all of these to us now and what part will they play in our lives in the future?'

10

Cologne

One evening over dinner David told Anna he would be making a visit to Cologne the following week.

'Klaus came to see me today, to give me details of a meeting he wants me to attend in Cologne. It's at a bank in which the Mustermann Corporation has considerable financial interest.'

'I'm sure you will do that very well,' Anna said. 'When will you be away?'

'I need to go on Thursday, for a meeting or meetings on Friday. I will go by train. Klaus has already given me the tickets.'

'I'm sorry I will not be able to join you. I have meetings booked for Friday to see a number of clients about changes to their accounts.'

'That's OK. What I thought you could do is catch a train after you finish work on Friday. In fact I've asked

Klaus to book a room with a double bed in a hotel near the station for Thursday, Friday and Saturday nights. I was hoping you would come along. Then we could look around the city on Saturday and travel back Sunday,' said David.

'You have made careful plans, haven't you? Just make sure you are the only one using the bed on Thursday night!' she said. 'I do so love Cologne. It holds special memories for me.'

'What sort of memories? asked David.

'Oh! It's such a magical city. I can show you many exciting places. I look forward to joining you. Don't forget what I said about Thursday night!' David smiled and raised his eyebrows.

David set off on Thursday afternoon. When he arrived in Cologne he walked the few steps from the station to the hotel and checked in. The lady in reception spoke first, in excellent English.

'Good afternoon, sir,' she said. 'You are most welcome.'

'Thank you,' said David. As she processed his papers, David guessed that she was in her forties or early fifties. Each time she spoke she had this engaging smile and she was blessed with an amazing personality.

'I'm right in thinking you come from the UK?'

'Yes, but now I live in Stuttgart.'

'Also, warum sprechen Sie nur auf Englisch?' she enquired.

'So how is it you speak only in English?' she enquired.

'Ich kann Deutsch sprechen, aber Sie haben mit mir zuerst auf Englisch gesprochen,' he said.

'I can speak German, but you spoke to me first in English,' he said.

'Yes, I think I did. So how is it that you, an Englishman, live in Germany?'

'I lived in England all my life until nearly two years ago. That was when my wife died and I managed to get a job in Stuttgart. I'm here to meet with officials from the bank across the square tomorrow. Would you recommend any of the local restaurants for a meal later?'

'No, not really,' she replied. 'I will have to leave it to you to choose and there is, of course, a very good restaurant in the hotel. I am sorry I will not be able to join you. I am on duty tonight.' David thanked her and made his way to his room.

David found a restaurant near the hotel. It was so hot he decided to eat outside. The meal and wine were excellent and put him in good spirits for the next day. As he wandered around some of the streets, he was surprised to see a number of men sleeping rough, either on the ground or on park benches. Other men, women and children were begging near the cathedral and railway station. David wondered if some of these were migrants or refugees, who had reached Europe by boat after fleeing wars in Syria and Iraq.

David went to reception to wish good night to the bubbly receptionist, only to find a man was on duty.

'*Ich erwartete eine junge Dame hier zu sein, um sie einen guten Abend zu wünschen,*' he said.

'*I expected a young lady to be here, for me to wish her good night,*' he said.

'*Entschuldigen Sie, mein Herr. Sie hat die Arbeit vor einiger Zeit verlassen,*' the man replied.

'*I'm sorry, sir. She finished work some time ago,*' the man replied.

David bade farewell to the receptionist and made his way towards the stairs.

David's instructions from Klaus were to arrive at the bank in good time, for a meeting scheduled to begin at 10 o'clock. He arrived early and a member of staff showed him to an interview room. He sat himself down in what looked to him like the visitor's chair and waited for someone to come and speak with him. David had plenty of time to notice the details of the table, desk, chairs and cupboards, together with the electronic equipment. It reminded him of a game he used to play when he was a boy. He was given a minute to scrutinise a picture and then he had to write down everything he could remember about it. Even after several minutes nobody came and after several minutes more. When a man in a grey suit came in expressing apologies for the delay, David took a quick glance at his watch and discovered thirty minutes had passed from the time the meeting was scheduled to start.

'I'm sorry nobody has been in to talk with you so far,' the man said, 'but Herr Strauss has been detained.

In the meantime I would like to offer you some coffee while you are waiting.'

'I will have a white coffee with no sugar, please,' David replied. He was amazed at the delay. The bank officials had been given more than a week's notice of the papers to be presented at the meeting. David kept his thoughts to himself for the present. The young man promptly returned with the coffee.

Another forty-five minutes elapsed before anyone else came to see David. This time it was an older man carrying a number of folders, from which sheets of paper protruded in a disorderly fashion. David made a snap judgement about the man and his attitude to what he was carrying. He plonked himself in the chair opposite David and proceeded to explain the results for the first six months of 2015. He said he would go and leave David to study the figures and write a report for the meeting to be held after lunch. As he made for the door David called him back.

'This is completely unacceptable,' he said. 'I have been here since 10 o'clock to receive and discuss the finances and put together a report to be signed and dated as a true record of the accounts for this bank. Now you tell me this will not happen until this afternoon.'

'I apologise that I was delayed,' said Herr Strauss. 'I was told you had all day, so the meeting did not need to start until the afternoon. I suggest you examine the results for January to June 2015 and write your report. Then after lunch we can meet at 14.00, to sign off these accounts.' David reluctantly agreed.

The accounts were correct and David wrote a brief report to this effect. He also commented on the considerable waste of time there had been. Both men signed and dated the accounts and David's report and three copies were run off, one for the bank and two for the Mustermann Corporation. They shook hands and David left the bank. He was fuming because of what had happened. It was this kind of sloppy behaviour that had caused banks to lose millions of dollars. This would not have been tolerated at IFS. All I am, he thought, is a highly-paid courier. The information I am carrying could have been sent by email or post. The only advantage of me taking it is that it should arrive safely.

David returned to the hotel for a drink and then had a shower and changed. He went to the platform shortly before Anna's train was due to arrive. When it came, she was not on it. He sent her a text to find out where she was.

'Sorry,' Anna replied. 'I missed the train. I should be there in an hour.'

Next morning it was hot when David and Anna emerged from the hotel.

'Let me show you the Cathedral first,' said Anna. 'It's a fascinating building. It was nearing completion after six hundred years and then within a short time it was damaged by bombs during the Second World War. Not all of it was destroyed; the twin towers were left intact.

As they walked around the Cathedral Anna described to David the stories depicted in the stained glass windows and explained the Stations of the Cross.

'You seem to be very knowledgeable about this,' he said.

'It was all part of my upbringing, along with other children who were brought up in West Germany. Don't you know Bible stories about Moses, David and Goliath, and the birth and death of Jesus?'

'Not really. I've never had much time for God!'

'So who or what gives purpose to your life, David?'

'I do! I don't need God.'

'So what do you think happens when people die?'

'People die and that's it. There's nothing else! I had to think about this when Emma died. I came to the conclusion that the funeral we had for her was just a good way to say 'Goodbye'. What do you think?'

'I believe there must be something after death. There are so many Christians in the world they can't all have got it wrong!'

This conversation stalled as they moved from the darkness within the Cathedral to the brightness of the sun outside. The square in front of the Cathedral was thronging with people. It was a meeting place for many. In some places there were little groups of musicians playing to small audiences. It was a place where there was freedom for all; nobody told anybody else what to do or say; it was a complete mix of cultures.

'I think this is wonderful,' Anna said.

In another part of the square someone had erected an Italian flag and beside it people had written various slogans and comments; there were a number of people who were pro or anti the migrants from Iraq, Syria and North Africa; another slogan read 'Free Palestine'.

Anna then led the way to the bridge that carries the railway and pedestrians over the Rhine towards the observation platform called the Cologne Triangle. On the fence separating the railway from the footbridge there were thousands of locks of all sizes, shapes and colours.

'You will have to explain the meaning of all those locks,' said David.

'Lovers pledge themselves to each other by securing a lock to the fence and throwing the key into the river.'

'What a lovely idea! We should do it.'

'But we don't have a lock,' she said.

'We could go and buy one.'

'I think it's all a bit unnecessary. There are millions of lovers throughout the world who love each other dearly without attaching a lock to a fence to demonstrate that love. They love each other and that's it. There's no need for anything else.'

David thought it was sad that Anna wouldn't take action to show her love for him in this way.

They had coffee served by friendly staff in a café at the foot of the Triangle. A lift took them twenty-eight floors to the top in a matter of seconds. The cost of three

Euros for an adult for this trip seemed very reasonable. Anna and David easily picked out the Cathedral and the River Rhine. They could also identify several churches in Cologne and picked out the cities of Dortmund and Bonn. David took lots of photos. He admitted to Anna he was anxious when near the edge of the viewing platform, in spite of having the security of some high plate-glass.

'Perhaps that's the reason you don't like skiing,' Anna scoffed. 'It's because you don't like the height from which you start!'

'Very funny,' replied David with a scowl.

Later David suggested an open-topped bus trip around the city and Anna readily agreed. It was so hot they elected to sit on the top deck.

'Can we find time to look at some of the places again?' asked David. 'One I'm really interested in is the Roman Museum.'

'Yes, we could go and have a look inside.'

After that David was keen to take some photos in the centre of Cologne. He particularly wanted some shots of the Cathedral and others showing Anna in various locations in the city. Now Cathedral Square was busier than it had been earlier in the day. Added to the previous entertainment, there were now singers and dancers, together with groups chanting slogans, such as one might hear at a football match. David found it difficult to take photos under these circumstances. There was so much jostling at times that he feared for the safety of Anna and himself. At times it was hard to hold on to his equipment. He decided it wasn't possible to edit photos as he took them. This process would have to wait until he was back at the hotel.

'I've managed to get some good pictures of you,' he said. 'Quite surprising, bearing in mind the conditions under which they were taken.' A little later he let out an expletive. 'I don't believe that!' he exclaimed. 'You remember that girl I told you about who was begging in Metz? She's on a couple of shots I took outside the Cathedral.

'I don't think it will be the same girl,' replied Anna. David showed her the photos. 'She may look like the same girl, but she resembles thousands of Eastern European girls. Only you saw the girl in Metz and you didn't take a photo of her. You've no way of proving it's one and the same girl.'

'But look at the way she's posing, looking straight at the camera. It's as if in these two photos she is the subject. Nothing else matters, neither the Cathedral, nor anyone else.'

'The only thing that can pose for a photo,' said Anna, 'is a person who knows she is being taken. The Cathedral doesn't! Nor do all the people who are not aware there's a photographer about.'

'That's exactly what I'm saying. She recognised me and looked straight into the camera, so I got a good photo of her. I bet you a hundred Euros that this girl here,' David said pointing to the photo, 'is the same girl I saw in Metz.'

'But we've no way of proving or disproving this, so there's no contest; your money is safe,' said Anna spreading her arms as though celebrating victory.

David was annoyed that Anna didn't believe him and seemed to be suggesting he was making up a story that the two girls were, in fact, the same girl. Why would he do that? What had he to gain? He was determined to have the last word. 'Perhaps you will believe me when we see her again somewhere else. What will you say then?' he asked.

Anna remained silent as her considered best response to what David had said.

11

Turmoil

Shortly after David and Anna returned from the UK something happened that was to bring into sharper focus the plight of refugees from Syria and Iraq. The picture of three year-old Alan Kurdi lying dead on a Turkish beach was shown on TV news programmes and in newspapers across the world. That picture, and the one showing a Turkish soldier carrying the dead child away from the beach, served as a wake-up call to the world about the plight of migrants and refugees.

'That's awful,' said Anna, as she and David continued to stare at the television. 'It looks as if I'll be going away a few more times yet' David frowned. He knew it had to be done, but he didn't like it when Anna went away and he was left on his own. As Anna predicted, she received the call to go a few days later.

'It's such a shame,' said David. 'Just as we were getting our lives back on track and sorting out our relationship, you get called away.'

'I know; I feel the same way. I love you and I would rather stay here with you, but I have to go when I'm needed. I hope it won't be for long and I can be back in your arms again soon.'

'I look forward to that, more than you know,' he said. He went over and held her close to him and they threw themselves into a passionate kissing session, which moved from the lounge into the bedroom. There they removed their clothes and enjoyed a wonderful time of intimacy.

'I don't think you realise what that does for me,' David said.

'I think I do. Don't you think it does something for me too?'

'I hope you won't be away too long and then we can enjoy that experience again.'

Over a meal David and Anna talked over their plans for the next few days and further into the future. 'One thing we must do is go over to the UK and spend time with my family,' he said.

'Yes we must,' Anna said. 'We've been so busy that we haven't been able to find the time. I'll leave you to arrange this. The other thing we need to do, when things settle down again, is to have a good holiday. I suggest it should be partly for skiing and partly for sightseeing. I think we should go to Switzerland.

I haven't been there for a long time. I will book up for sometime early in 2016.'

After Anna had gone away, David decided he must try to organise his life. Up to the present he felt like a juggler attempting to give a polished performance, but in danger of dropping one of the balls at any time. It was a demanding job to keep his fellow directors and board members up to date with the financial state of the Mustermann Corporation in challenging times. The continuing slump in the price of oil meant that overall profits were falling. He was managing to keep abreast of the businesses already within the Mustermann Corporation and those that were potential partners and had enquired about joining. However, at no time did David think he had got on top of this. He had discussed this with Franz on more than one occasion and his response was always the same.

'If they keep to the guidelines, they're in; if not, they're out. We can't have businesses sitting on the fence and messing us about,' Franz said.

David thought this sounded fine in theory, but it often didn't work out in practice. There would be a number of firms constantly moving in or dropping out and many would fail to communicate from one month to another. David also raised with Franz the situation of some of the banks in particular, that arranged a meeting that took the best part of a day to produce a financial report, when it could have been sent electronically, with far less expenditure of time and money. Franz said he would look into this and he would speak to David about it sometime in the future.

About a week later Franz sent David an invitation to join him and Klaus to a meeting over lunch, which he readily accepted. He assumed it had something to do with his suggestion for passing on monthly financial reports electronically.

When David was shown into the dining room he did wonder if he should have made more effort to dress formally rather than casually. The table was set for three people, but the attention to detail would not have been out of place for a large formal banquet. The floral decoration at the end of the table was exquisite. He need not have concerned himself about his appearance. Franz and Klaus had adopted the same casual style as he had.

The food was beautifully presented and tasted delicious. 'It's good to have a special meal in the middle of a working day from time to time,' said Franz. 'It gives the opportunity for us to talk business in a relaxed atmosphere while we enjoy some great food.' As he finished saying this, he got up from the table and uncorked a bottle of red wine. He presented it to David, who took a sip and said, 'Das ist gut!' Franz then poured three glasses.

David expressed agreement with Franz about having the occasional special meal and he thanked Klaus and Franz for inviting him. During almost a year of working for the Mustermanns, it was the first time he had been invited to such a meal. He wondered about the timing of this invitation.

Conversation was wide-ranging and it was conducted in German and English. 'Die Welt ist in einem schlimmen Zustand,' said Klaus. 'Es gibt erbitterte Kämpfe in Irak, Syrien und anderen Ländern des Mittleren Ostens und in Nord und Zentralafrika. Sie herumstreifen ungehindert, diejenigen die im Namen von ISIS kämpfen. Die Zeit geht vorbei und es gibt immer mehr Flüchtlinge und Migranten, die nach Europa zu reisen versuchen, um das Blutvergießen zu entkommen.'

'The world is in a terrible state,' said Klaus. 'There is fighting in Iraq and Syria, in other countries of the Middle East, and in North and Central Africa. People who support ISIS seem to roam about unchecked and there are more refugees and migrants trying to travel to Europe to escape the bloodshed.'

'We have offered help by donating money and we have encouraged Anna to be involved in helping child refugees,' said Franz. David thought it was Anna's initial involvement that led the Mustermann Corporation to get involved. However, he did think it was good to have financial and practical support from the Corporation.

'Coalition bombing is impacting ISIS,' Klaus said, 'and Russia joining in with the bombing of Syria has tipped the balance since one of its passenger jets was shot down over Egypt.'

David interrupted with a financial observation. 'One of the worst developments from a Mustermann viewpoint is the dramatic fall in the price of oil. Another is the slowing down of markets in China, at a time when we were investing heavily in that country.' Klaus and

Franz agreed with David's observations, but brought the discussion back to the problem of refugees and migrants.

'It's the huge numbers that are increasing the problem,' said Klaus.

'But what can we do when our Chancellor is encouraging more people to come to Germany?' said Franz.

'Two steps must be taken,' David suggested. 'One is to stop the fighting in Syria and Iraq and the other is to prevent people from getting to Europe.'

Klaus looked intently at David and once he had finished speaking, he addressed issues of importance to the Mustermann Corporation. 'Have you managed to obtain current statements of finance that you requested from all those businesses where we might have future involvement?' he asked.

'Most of them,' David replied.

'What about those that are struggling?' asked Franz.

'This is more difficult. Some reply, others don't.'

Franz continued his questions. 'Which ones don't? Are they the ones we visit on a regular basis, or those which send in their statements monthly?'

'It is usually the ones that send in their statements,' David said.

'So this goes against your suggestion that we obtain results electronically and no longer do visits, wouldn't you agree?'

David remained silent. Then realising he had shot himself in the foot, he said, 'It would seem sensible to continue doing visits at the present time!'

'Thank you Mr. Burrows,' said Franz.

'There is one other innovation we would like to introduce as soon as possible,' said Klaus. David felt deflated after his previous verbal defeat, so he looked forward with a certain amount of trepidation to what Klaus was about to say. 'We feel it would be good to set you a number of assignments to guide your work over the coming months.' David's heart sank. His mind went back more than thirty years, to when he was sixteen. A new examination system called the Certificate of Secondary Education (CSE) had been introduced, to help those pupils who found it difficult to obtain qualifications by sitting 'O' levels. Instead of sitting one or two exam papers for each subject, there was a considerable emphasis on coursework. Each CSE subject required a number of pieces of coursework to be completed. These were called Assignments;. 'xxxxxx Assignments' David and his mates called them. A large amount of written work had to be submitted to gain the equivalent of an 'O' level. For one whose presentation skills left something to be desired, David would have preferred to cram his head with facts and sit written papers. Hence the derogatory terms used to describe Assignments!

'Perhaps there will be six assignments over the next six months,' Klaus said. 'Maybe you will have a week to complete each assignment. That would include your preparation and research, a fact-finding visit and a final report. I'm sure you will be able to fill the rest of your time suitably!'

David felt somewhat numb after this final discussion. Sadly it had taken the shine off an excellent meal, which had been pushed to the recesses of his mind. He did remember to thank Klaus and Franz for a splendid lunch before taking his leave. He couldn't remember any mention of assignments in his job description, but Anna would have said they were in the small print somewhere! It probably also said that changes could be made to the conditions of employment at any time and that could include changes in salary!

The other thing that Klaus said that surprised David, if he understood correctly, was that he would have a week allotted to each assignment, but it might only take two days to complete. The rest was free time. Now that sounded interesting, or was it some clever ploy to break him into redundancy slowly?

Anna's time away followed the same pattern as on the previous occasion. David heard nothing from her until shortly before she was due back, when he received a brief text, informing him of her time of arrival. On that same day David had a meeting with Franz, who gave him details of his first assignment.

'As you know, the Mustermann Corporation is seeking to expand the work of its operations. It would be good to add a firm from the drinks industry to our portfolio. Klaus and I have talked about this for some time. It has now come to our attention that a Scottish whisky distillery would welcome support from a financial institution, to establish its business on a firmer foundation. We have made the initial contact and you are now to investigate a deal. This will be your first assignment and I trust it will be successful. I will arrange your flights and hotel – we have a number of contacts, so we can achieve considerable savings.

'Could I ask which week this will be?' asked David.

'Next week, 5th to 9th October,' Franz replied. 'You can get a return flight from Stuttgart to Glasgow.'

'What I would like to do,' said David, 'is to fly to Glasgow on Monday 5th. Then do all the transactions with the distillery on Tuesday and Wednesday, 6th and 7th October. Then I would like to drive to North Yorkshire to visit my brother-in-law. That's Emma, my former wife's brother. Then I could fly back from Leeds-Bradford on Friday 9th.'

'I'm sure that can all be booked for you and I will arrange for you to stay in a suitable hotel on Thursday night.'

'I thought that was what Klaus intended when he spoke about assignments at our recent lunchtime meeting. It will work out well for me,' David said. 'I've not seen this brother-in-law before.'

'OK. I will get all these bookings made and tickets delivered to you on Saturday. Then you can be off on Monday. Do have a good weekend.'

As David walked away from Franz's office, he realised what he had just agreed to. Anna would be arriving back in two days time and two days after that he would be leaving for Scotland. At least they would have part of the weekend together. Although this was not ideal, it was better than nothing. They would have to make the most of the time they had. As he pondered the arrangements for the weekend David asked himself whether it was by chance that the arrangements had worked out the way they had, or was it planned to be that way? He did wonder!

Anna arrived on time, but as before, she looked pale and exhausted. She said nothing about what she had done during her time away. She spent much of her time asleep.

'I'm sorry I'm going to have to spoil the celebration for your homecoming,' David confessed. 'I have an assignment to complete in Scotland next week and I fly out on Monday morning.'

'That's OK. I'm sure you didn't plan it deliberately.'

'I didn't,' he said. 'Could someone else have planned it that way for me? It seems a bit too much of a coincidence that two days after you arrive home, I'm sent off to the UK for a week! I've been in touch with Steve and Jo and they've given me directions how to find John, Emma's brother. I look forward to meeting up with him.'

'Perhaps you are being over-suspicious about things that are happening in your life at the moment. Or maybe, just maybe, you have been very clever and discovered somebody else's plan. At least I can have time to recuperate and get myself into the routine at the bank by the time you return from Scotland. Then we can celebrate!'

12

Scotland

David woke early and Anna hardly stirred, so there was to be no passionate send off. He clambered into his pre-booked taxi and made the airport in good time. He experienced a smooth take-off, a pleasant three-and-a-half hour journey, and a soft landing at Glasgow International Airport. He collected his car and set out on the A814. He couldn't remember the last time he had visited Scotland, but as he headed North West and saw the hills and lochs, all the nostalgic memories came flooding back. The weather was somewhat overcast, but there was still sufficient brightness for him to appreciate the splendour and beauty of the scenery. Lochs Lomond, Fyne and Awe came and went, like long-lost friends. David stopped at Oban, which had been the starting point for holidays to the Western Isles in the past. He drove south on the A816 and then along the shore of Loch Awe and via Dumbarton back to Glasgow. The car's Sat Nav had directed him into the hotel's car park. He felt pleased that he had been able to experience the beauty of Scotland once again. He sent a text to Anna, while he still remembered, saying he had arrived safely.

David had a shower and changed before going down to the bar for a drink. There was one other man standing at the bar and David went over and introduced himself.

'Pleased to meet you,' the other man replied. 'I'm Mike. I notice you are driving a hire car, so I'm guessing you're not local.'

'You're right,' said David. 'I'm British, but I now live in Stuttgart in Germany.'

'So what brings you to this part of Scotland?'

'Whisky,' David answered with a wry smile. 'I'm not intending to buy loads or get drunk on it. I'm the Financial Director for a corporation interested in providing a local distillery with some capital to help it expand. At the same time it would be good to add a whisky distillery to our portfolio. So what do you do?' David asked Mike.

Before he had time to answer, the bar door swung open and a lady and man entered. Mike stepped forward and introduced himself and David. 'We were just getting acquainted,' he said. 'David had just told me he was looking for a suitable whisky distillery to acquire. So what are your names?'

'I'm Tony,' said the other man. 'We're not a couple, as you may have thought. We just happened to come through the door at the same time!'

'I'm Wendy,' said the lady. 'I confirm I'm not Tony's wife!' Everyone laughed.

David found out what the two newcomers wanted to drink and ordered them at the bar. 'Shall we take it easy,' he said, leading the way to a collection of chairs in one corner of the room.

Looking at Mike, David said, 'Now tell as what business you are in.'

'I'm a salesman for sports equipment and at present I'm visiting golf courses in this part of Scotland, hoping to sell some items of equipment.'

Wendy was the next to speak, seemingly to get her turn over and done with. 'I'm a Senior Executive of an oil company and I live in Edinburgh. I'm born and bred Scottish and a member of the SNP.'

Tony completed the list of profiles. 'I'm Senior Executive of a hotel chain,' he said, 'but not the one this hotel is in,' he added quickly.

After a pause David was the first to speak, directing his words to Wendy. 'The drop in the price of oil has probably done irreparable damage to your business this year.'

'Yes it has; more than a little.'

'I'm aware of this with my corporation,' said David. 'We have considerable investments in the oil industry and these are not so profitable this year as they were a year ago.'

Tony spoke to Wendy, 'In spite of the plummeting price of oil, you're still in favour of Scottish devolution,' he said.

'I want to see Scotland as a country in its own right; setting its own budget, raising its own taxes, passing its own laws, and not being run from Westminster any longer,' she said.

'In spite of a drop in the price of oil?' queried Mike.

'Yes, in spite of that.'

David turned the discussion to a subject that had exercised his thoughts a great deal since the General Election. 'David Cameron has said he will hold an in/out referendum by 2017, so the British people can vote if they want the UK to remain in Europe or leave. What do we think about this?'

Wendy said she thought it best to remain in the EU, but she expected Scotland would be a separate member state from the rest of the UK. Mike said he wanted the UK to stay in the EU, mainly because coming out might adversely affect his business. Tony said he was uncertain. He thought European countries should stick together, but this could open up the UK to more migrants and attacks by ISIS. David concluded discussion on this particular topic.

'I have experience of what is happening across Europe at the moment,' he said. 'The government in Germany is keen to welcome anyone, but more and more

German people are speaking out against this. As things stand at the moment migrants are free to move from country to country, because of the open borders policy that exists in the EU. My partner works for the EU, trying to help refugee children cope with what is happening to them as they move on day after day. The main part of her role is to make sure these children get some education. Although I can appreciate all the arguments for staying in because of the trade links, on balance I think it would be better if the UK leaves the EU. It would make our country safer and it would be less costly.'

Tony asked, 'Are we all having a meal?' The other three grunted or nodded to confirm they were. 'Can I suggest we order our meals and drinks and sit at one table to resume our discussion?' All agreed. Once the food arrived the conversation didn't sparkle as it had done previously. The scope was widened to include sport, women's rights, global warming and changes in education. At the end of the evening everyone agreed it had been great to meet in this way. With handshakes all round, they wished each other profitable business the next day.

David rose early the next morning. Anna had warned against having cooked breakfasts if he wanted to keep his weight down, so he had a Continental-style breakfast. He set the Sat Nav for the distillery he would be visiting and made good time in travelling there, in spite of the wet and windy conditions.

Mr McIntyre, the CEO at the distillery was waiting for David to arrive. He shook him warmly by the hand saying, 'You are a most welcome visitor to our distillery today. Please come with me to my office.' There he explained to David the programme for the day. Then Mr McIntyre rang for two managers at the plant. 'Please take Mr Burrows on a tour of the distillery,' he said.

David found the whole process of making whisky fascinating and he asked many questions. 'I've never been a whisky drinker,' he said, 'apart from the occasional tot for medicinal purposes! I had no idea how whisky was made and the effect different grains, waters, and oak casks have on the finished product.' At the end of the tour he was returned to Mr McIntyre's office, to have lunch with the boss.

'Would you take a wee dram with your lunch?' Mr McIntyre asked.

'I'd be delighted, but best make that a very wee dram,' David replied.

'I'll leave you to put your own water in,' the boss said.

Over lunch David found out more about the CEO's hopes for a link with the Mustermann Corporation. 'As I see it,' David observed, 'you don't want a complete sell-out to the Mustermann Corporation, but rather a percentage of the shares would be sold to us. Have you any idea how many?'

Mr McIntyre looked more serious than he had been so far. He picked up his glass and had a sip. 'Perhaps twenty-five percent.' David had been briefed by Franz to explore the possibility of a thirty percent share transfer, so twenty-five percent was near enough to negotiate on. After further discussion the two men agreed that the exact figure would be finalised later. That would be for Klaus and Franz to conclude a deal with Mr McIntyre.

David went on to enquire about the Financial Statements for the distillery over the past five years. 'These are all available for you,' replied Mr McIntyre. 'I will pass them on before you leave.'

'I see you are looking for a Financial Director,' David commented.

'Yes we are. Are you interested?'

'I have a very good job at the moment, but who knows what might happen in the future?'

'I will bear you in mind,' said Mr McIntyre. 'If you come back to my office we can have a cup of tea and I will pass on the financial papers to you. I will put in details of the post that is being advertised.' The two men indulged in small talk while drinking their tea.

Then David thanked Mr McIntyre who handed over the various papers. 'It has been a very informative day. I'm sure it will be productive for both of our businesses,' he said. With that he shook hands and left. He considered the whole operation to be efficiently run. Mr McIntyre was smart and pleasant, the sort of person it would be good to work for.

On arriving back at the hotel David freshened himself up and went to the bar. Apart from a couple perched on bar stools and deep in conversation, the room was empty. He thought he would wait to see if any of the other guests he had dined with the previous evening showed up. When the barman took his order, he asked about the three others.

'They all checked out this morning,' came the reply.

'In that case I'll have to eat alone,' said David, as he went and took a seat in the dining area of the bar.

When planning the itinerary for his trip to Scotland David decided a visit to Edinburgh must be included somewhere on the tour. He could do that the next day and spend the night in a hotel. Then on Thursday he would make his way south to North Yorkshire and look up John. He had left a message on his answering machine, but he would have to ring him on the journey to confirm the arrangements.

David had fond memories of Edinburgh and these came flooding back as he walked the streets of the city. He thought Anna would have loved Princes Street, if she was anything like Emma. A mixture of showery rain and gusty winds was not ideal weather for sightseeing. He took a long coffee break mid-morning to get some respite from the elements and had a pub lunch washed down with a pint of McEwan's Amber. David did manage to catch a glimpse of a distant TV screen that showed the refugee crisis was still going on.

He booked into a hotel early and spent time relaxing in the lounge. He sent Anna a text, 'Yest visit went well. Going see Jn 2moro. Dxx', but he received no reply.

The next day it rained steadily on the first part of the journey, but it had stopped by the time David reached Yorkshire. He phoned his brother-in-law, 'Hello is that John?'

'Yes. You must be David. I'm looking forward to meeting you, another member of my new family.'

The sun came out as David travelled through the North York Moors National Park to give the semblance of a pleasant autumn day. John was outside anticipating David's arrival. They gave each other a hug.

'It's good to meet you,' John said. 'Thank you for calling in to see me.'

'I couldn't do otherwise,' David replied, 'as I'm travelling south from Scotland. I just had to call in and meet you. Isn't it beautiful round here? I don't think I would like it in the middle of winter though.'

'So we're brothers-in-law,' John said. 'I knew about you from our Emma when she was in Manchester, but we never actually met. C'mon let's go inside and we can talk over a cup of coffee.'

'You knew about me,' David said, 'but I knew absolutely nothing about you. When Emma died and we were sorting through her things we found this photograph of her with a young man, who turned out to be you!'

'I understand that photo caused you, in particular, some concern.'

'It did, but that's all in the past. One regret I have is that we didn't find that photograph two years ago.

Then perhaps we might have found you before Emma died.'

'I think that would have been very unlikely. It was our Emma's death that caused you and the family to search amongst her possessions that led you to me.'

'I'm glad we have met up,' David said, putting an arm round John's shoulder. 'We must keep in touch.'

'I'll try,' John said, 'but I'm not the world's best communicator!'

'I'd best be off,' said David, starting to get emotional again.

'Where are you off to?'

'I'm driving to Leeds-Bradford airport, where I'll stay in a hotel for the night. Then tomorrow I fly off to Germany.'

'Germany?' queried John. Is that where you live?'

'Yes, in Stuttgart. I work for a large firm and I was sent to check out a Scottish whisky distillery, with a view to my firm buying some shares.'

'Sounds an interesting job, but I can't say I would like a job like that because I wouldn't. I've never flown and I like living in Yorkshire.'

David didn't mention Anna when he spoke about life in Germany. He thought that may have exposed a raw nerve, causing John to hold a grudge against him for marrying someone else after his sister died.

They had one final hug by the gate and David got into his car and drove off. He headed for the A1(M) and arrived at the airport hotel in good time. He had three things on his mind – catching his flight to Stuttgart in the morning; passing on the information about the whisky distillery to Klaus and Franz; meeting up with Anna again. Needless to say, his reunion with Anna was uppermost in his mind. He checked his mobile before getting into bed. There was still no reply to the text he sent Anna the previous day.

A taxi dropped David in the square at the heart of Stuttgart. He noticed a light was on in the flat as he made his way home. He unlocked the door and Anna rushed forward to give him a passionate kiss to welcome him home.

'It's good to have you back,' she said. 'I've booked up a holiday in Switzerland for the last two weeks in February. The first week will be in an apartment in Grindelwald and we will do mainly skiing that week. During the second week in Mürren we will stay in a hotel and do lots of sightseeing.

Although David would be thrilled to holiday in Switzerland when the time came, his immediate preoccupation was to get his hands on Anna and feel her body pressed close to his. 'It's special to be in your welcoming arms once again,' he said. As he hugged her tighter and examined her face he thought she looked fine. The sparkle was back and all the signs of exhaustion and stress had disappeared.

'Why didn't you reply to my text?' he asked.

'I didn't know I had one,' Anna replied. 'Now you can tell me everything you want to say face to face, without the need for a mobile. I've made Eintopf with a very nice red wine to go with it. Then after that, I'm your dessert!'

'I look forward to whatever you have to offer! Shall we start now?'

13

Grindelwald

A new year began some weeks ago and still nothing had been said about David's trip to Scotland and the negotiations he had started, to acquire shares in the whisky distillery. After another week he received an email summoning him to attend an urgent meeting with Klaus and Franz. When David arrived he experienced the same anxious feelings he remembered from his school days, when he was summoned to the headmaster's study. His gentle knock on the office door was greeted with a loud, 'Come in!' As he entered he noticed that Franz and his father were seated on the far side of the table and there was a solitary chair arranged so he would face them. This confirmed to

David that he was going to be in the dock for something he was presently unaware of.

'Sit down, Mr Burrows,' said Franz. David wondered what had brought on the change to a formal greeting. Klaus leaned across to Franz and said something behind his hand, but there was no way David could hear what was said. However, Klaus' expression revealed something about his secret message. Franz continued to adopt the same hostile attitude.

'It is now more than three months since you visited the whisky distillery in Scotland,' he said. 'We still haven't had a report from you. Why is this?'

David thought quickly. He was certain he had filed a report. 'I produced a report within a few days of my visit.'

'So where is it?' demanded Franz.

'I filed it under Scotland whisky distilleries.' Klaus and Franz turned to their screens and found the report.

'Why didn't you say something about this?' asked Franz. 'It would have saved us from making numerous enquiries while you have been away.'

David's confidence was rising as time went on and he was going to make the most of being right. 'I sent you both an email in early November, attaching my report; the one you have just found.'

Klaus and Franz looked crestfallen as they exchanged glances, but Franz wasn't going to accept blame for what happened. He continued in the same bombastic tone, 'I hope you realise I had to ring Mr

McIntyre, to find out the substance of your discussions. It's not good for me to have to ring up an organisation with whom we are hoping to do business and ask what happened during the meeting, all because one of our employees has failed to report back to us.'

David said nothing. He didn't need to. He knew and they knew he was right and he didn't have to do anything to prove it. Franz continued on another tack. 'When we sent you to Scotland,' he said, 'We asked you to try for a minimum stake of 30% and hopefully more, but I see your discussions failed to go beyond 25%.'

'I thought that was a good figure to use as the basis for further negotiation.' David said. 'Mr McIntyre appreciated that it would be up to you two to hammer out a final deal with him.'

Klaus pointed to a piece of paper on his desk. This reminded Franz to continue with his interrogatory style and throw in a touch of sarcasm for good measure. Franz continued, 'When I spoke to Mr McIntyre he told me he had spoken to you about the Financial Director post he had available at that time. David felt sad and annoyed by this revelation. He had considered Mr McIntyre to be a person of honesty and integrity. However, the fact that he had told David's current bosses that there was a post at his distillery in which David had shown interest meant the Scotsman fell rapidly in David's estimation of him as a good employer.

'I said I had a very good job at present,' David explained. 'I thought no more about the job and I deleted details from my memory and my PC's memory.'

'But you were initially interested,' Franz countered. David considered further comment unnecessary.

As the meeting drew towards a close, Franz tried a tactic he'd used on previous occasions, particularly when things hadn't gone well for the Mustermanns, as had happened earlier in this meeting. It involved loading an employee with so much extra work that he or she would wish they hadn't gained the upper hand in the previous skirmishes. Franz said, 'You will remember you are doing various assignments over the next few months. I don't think we can count your first assignment as a success, so you will have opportunities to redeem yourself. This is the time of the year when banks, businesses and corporations are attempting to put their finances in order for their annual reports. We would like you to visit three banks that are under the Mustermann Corporation umbrella. They have done this before and they know what to expect. We want you to attend the next board meeting for each bank, one in Berlin, one in Heidelberg and one in Bonn; two in January and one in February. By the end of each board meeting you should make an assessment of the bank's suitability to remain in business with us and you should bring back the latest Statement of Account. You will need to write a report for each bank and file it within two days of your visit. We don't want another fiasco like we had with your previous assignment. So that's three assignments and another can be keeping us updated on existing and potential partners.'

When Franz had finished David was tempted to ask, 'Is that it, or have you forgotten something?' but he thought better of it. After all he wasn't the one using sarcasm. Compared with the previous occasion David had got off lightly. Why? Were they deliberately giving him less to do, so they could accuse him of working below par at a later date?

David shared with Anna over a meal what had happened to him earlier in the day. He said, 'I don't mind being criticised or even reprimanded for making a mistake or doing something wrong, but I'm not happy if I get the blame for someone else's mistake. Klaus and Franz hadn't found the report I'd filed, or the email I sent them telling them about it. Then they ring Mr McIntyre in Scotland to get his take on the meeting, apologising for me being incompetent. Did this happen to you when you worked for the Mustermanns?'

'I was in a different role to you,' said Anna. 'I didn't go out to visit clients in the same way that you do. I never went on my own and I was there principally to take notes and write reports. I did warn you things were likely to get worse. What you must understand is that Klaus and Franz are always right and they never make mistakes! You might be right sometimes, but certainly not all the time.'

'Towards the end of our meeting Franz drew attention to the assignments I have to do,' said David. 'He didn't think my first assignment was a success, so I've been given more, and then I can earn more brownie points and put me back in their good books! I have to visit three banks and sit in on their board meetings, then write reports. I have two this month and one in February. It doesn't look as though I'm going to be overworked.'

'Be careful,' replied Anna. 'You remember how long I took to finalise the accounts before I left the Mustermann's employment. That wasn't because I was slow. Far from it,' she said winking at David. 'It was because I did it as I was told and then one of them decided they didn't want it done that way and I had to start again! If you do find you have lots of spare time, you can help get things ready for going on holiday and you can arrange the route we'll take. To be honest I'm so busy at work I can't think about our holiday right now.'

'I had thought I would take the Merc,' said David. 'It will give us more travel options when we're in Grindelwald. When do we go?'

'Four weeks time,' she replied. 'One thing you might do is to find out what the weather is going to be like. So far many of the resorts haven't had their usual amount of snow.'

Anna continued to run herself ragged right up to the time they set off on holiday. David on the other hand felt rested and relaxed. He was looking forward to going away and having a break from work. After his experiences with Klaus and Franz, he couldn't get away fast enough!

It was overcast when David and Anna set off from Stuttgart. The traffic was moderate and they were able to make good progress.

'I don't know why you are going so fast,' said Anna. 'You can slow down a bit and then I would feel much safer.'

'I thought I would put some miles, sorry kilometres, behind us while we had the chance. We can stop for a coffee and comfort break sometime. I'm aiming to reach somewhere near Zurich before we stop for the night. Maybe we could get as far as Lucerne. It's ages since I've been there and I'd appreciate seeing its beauty again.'

The first hotel Anna tried had a vacancy. As it was getting cooler, they put off sightseeing around Lucerne until the next day.

'It's not as colourful around the lake as it was the last time I was here,' David said.

'What do you expect?' Anna replied rather abruptly. 'I'm sure the last time you were here was probably in summer and now we're only just coming out of winter. That's why the temperature is a lot lower than on your previous visit!'

Anna and David ambled around the old town holding hands. She was now more relaxed than she had been back in Stuttgart. From time to time she would grip his hand more tightly to remind him of her presence and David copied her action.

'We've got time to have a bite to eat before we leave Lucerne,' he said. 'Then we can do the last part of the journey this afternoon. It's not far and shouldn't take us long.' These words would come back to haunt David later.

'Oh no,' he exclaimed, as they travelled at a comfortable speed along the Autobahn.'

'What's wrong?' asked Anna.

'There's a dark blue car bearing down on me, going far faster than I am.' As the car came closer the driver moved into the next lane and slowed to the same speed as David's Merc and honked the horn loudly. A number of young people were hanging out of the rear windows and giving a variety of gestures as the honking continued.

'Do be careful,' warned Anna. 'Don't do anything silly so we crash. I think the driver is trying to challenge you to a race.'

'I'll just keep going at this speed and then I'll slow down slightly. It must have been a dream come true for the driver to come across another fast car he could race against.'

Still the honking and gestures continued and the young people were shouting, but it was impossible to hear the words. David could see from the signs that a road would be leaving the Autobahn shortly. He reduced his speed a little at a time, so he was no longer alongside the other vehicle. Then at the last minute he pulled his Merc off the Autobahn. The driver of the blue car was taken unawares and continued along the Autobahn. There was only light traffic on the main road and it occurred to David the other driver might reverse and take the exit he had taken.

'I hope I've lost him,' David said. 'I'll pull off and park just up here and we can go into the café.' Anna and

David scurried from the car to the cover of the café, breathing a sigh of relief.

'My heart is pounding and I'm almost struggling for breath,' said Anna.

'Me too. We'll take time having a coffee and I hope we've lost them.'

As they joined the refreshments queue, Anna moved close to David and in a soft voice asked, 'What sort of car was it?'

'A Subaru. Super Subaru some people call it. Modified to travel at high speed.'

'Those in the car were a varied bunch,' Anna observed, 'sporting clothes and hair of various colours.'

'And probably high on drugs, alcohol, or both. I hope we don't meet up with them again while we're in Switzerland.'

'You do have some interesting experiences with other cars when you are on holiday!' Anna said, reminding him of the accident that first caused them to meet up some eighteen months ago.

'I would like it to be known that neither of these incidents were caused by me,' David said with an air of defiance.

'I suggest we buy essentials from the store when we get to Grindelwald,' said Anna. 'Then we can find the apartment, unload the car and keep a low profile, for the rest of today anyway.'

After a meal, Anna and David spent time with their arms around each other and engaged in some mild kissing until they became so passionate that it had to be concluded in the bedroom. David was pleased Anna now seemed very relaxed and had left her hang-ups back home. Anna explained to David that some of the ski slopes wouldn't be open because there had been too little snow. 'We can go to some slopes, but they are likely to be very crowded,' she said. 'My suggestion is that we have a good exploration of Grindelwald tomorrow and we could take a trip on a train the next day while we wait for the snow.'

David was awake first the next morning and after having a shower and getting dressed, he went outside. It was colder than he expected and the melted snow had frozen on the car park and roads. He thought a brief circular walk would be quite enough in view of the low temperature and his inadequate clothing. He was more than a little concerned to find a blue Subaru in the car park, but he couldn't be certain it was the same one as they had seen the previous day. Loud music was emanating from one of the apartments and he hoped it was not one in close proximity to where he and Anna were staying and where she was still sleeping. As David continued to think about the noise, a well-dressed man came out of the apartments and got into the blue Subaru. After a few minor adjustments, he drove on to the road and disappeared from David's view. David thought it was very unlikely this man was associated with the blue Subaru and its riotous passengers seen yesterday. He therefore dismissed any connection from his mind. By this time he was almost back to his starting point and a few more steps took him back into the warmth of the apartment block.

The morning was spent looking around Grindelwald. Over lunch David and Anna talked about what they might do in the afternoon. 'There are ski lifts that could take us to short ski runs,' said Anna. 'At least it will give us a chance to practise some basic skiing before the snow arrives. When it does, everywhere will be crowded.'

'I'm all for that,' David said. 'It's nearly a year since we last had a skiing holiday and I'm sure it will show the first time I get on the snow. What are you going to suggest we do tomorrow?'

'I thought we would take the Jungfrau Express from Grindelwald to Jungfraujoch. We go on a variety of trains through some beautiful scenery. I know you've not been before and I'm sure you will find it an exhilarating experience.'

'I really look forward to that,' he said. 'What is it they call the Jungfrau? The Top of Europe?'

After lunch they went back to their apartment to change and pick up their equipment. They hired the rest in Grindelwald. David revelled in the opportunity to ski again and he couldn't wait to get on the snow. There were lots of people on the slopes above Grindelwald, all eager to get on their skis again. Young and old, short and tall, men and women, all behaving as if they had just been let out from school, shouting and laughing to one another.

'Isn't it brilliant,' said David. 'It's all coming back. Rather like riding a bike!'

'Do keep your concentration, otherwise you could get in somebody's way and get hit,' Anna warned.

After a couple of hours David had experienced all he wanted on this, his first practice session of the season. He came to a halt and left Anna to do some longer runs. As he stood there watching everyone else his mind was full of questions. He hoped he would still remember them when Anna returned.

'Are there ski marshals or stewards patrolling the slopes to ensure everyone keeps safe?' he asked.

'Not really. People are free to ski where they like.'

'But who are those wearing red ski jackets? I assumed they were marshals. Look over there,' David said, pointing. 'They have been looking around through binoculars and they have spent time looking in my direction.'

'Sometimes a group of skiers will wear the same colour, so they can identify each other more easily.' Anna said. 'I should have warned you not to do anything that might arouse suspicion and cause you to get arrested!'

'I'm OK so far,' David said, 'Nobody has come over and spoken to me.'

'But you don't know what notes they have jotted down about you!'

The next day was bright but cold. David couldn't think of enough superlatives to describe the train journey to Jungfraujoch and the walking tour he and Anna did at the top, under the shadow of the Jungfrau.

'I'm full of admiration for the engineers who were the first to build these railways with different tracks and trains,' he said. 'The views are simply stunning. The air is so fresh and clean up here. I've taken a number of photos, but they don't do justice to the actual views. As one who has been here before', David said looking at Anna, 'what is your favourite experience?'

'It's difficult to restrict myself to just one,' Anna said. 'The Ice Palace and the Panorama Experience are two of my favourites. On a clear day like today it's wonderful that we can also view the peaks in Germany and France.'

'Let's enjoy this beauty for a little while longer,' David said. 'After all I don't suppose I will see it again. I'm then going to suggest we travel back via Wengen and Lauterbrunnen. It will give us further stunning scenery.'

As David and Anna travelled downwards from the Jungfrau's heights, they were fascinated to watch the skiers who were also on the long downhill journey.

'I'm not sure I would fancy skiing so far downhill,' said David. 'Look over there,' he said pointing out of the train window. 'Who are those two skiers dressed in white?' he asked.

'Which ones? I can't see them.'

'The problem is the skiers don't follow the railway track all the time, so they get hidden behind buildings and bits of vegetation. There they are again. They've got rifles slung over their shoulders.'

Anna spoke to reduce the panic David was showing. 'They're perhaps taking part in a Biathlon event, where they have to combine cross-country skiing with rifle shooting,' she said.

'So what are the targets,' asked David, looking rather anxious.

'You have five shots at five circles. When you hit them all, you move on. If you miss, you get a time penalty. Don't look so worried!'

'I am worried. What happens if they are looking for a human target, maybe you or me?'

'Don't be so silly, David. They won't fire at you while you're on this train.'

He wasn't so easily convinced. However, he did start to feel better once the train had left the marksmen behind. He and Anna changed trains at Lauterbrunnen to travel back to Grindelwald. It had been a wonderful day, even though his stress-level had gone up with the sight of rifle-carrying skiers on the way back.

The snow that had been expected since the weekend fell in abundance that night. 'Wow,' said David. 'Look at that. It looks like some magical scene from a fairy tale. I know what we'll be doing today, tomorrow and the next day.'

'Just a warning,' said Anna. 'We need to pace ourselves and plan some relaxation as well as skiing.'

'It's good of you to think of the old man,' David said sarcastically. 'I know it's easier for younger and fitter skiers to recover after skiing, but I'll be sensible and listen to your words of advice. I know one thing I would really like to do before we return home.'

'What's that?' Anna asked.

'I'd like to have a go at paragliding. Will you join me?'

'I don't' think so. I love the thrill of downhill skiing, but I don't like the idea of coming down from the sky without a plane! You can go without me.'

David came up with a plan. ''We'll go skiing today...'

'Or until we can't ski any more,' interrupted Anna.

'Let's then have tomorrow off,' he said. 'We can spend the day in Interlaken. We can have a meal there. Then ski again on Friday. I can go paragliding while we're in Interlaken.'

'It's going to take longer than you think. It may take five minutes to descend, but it will take a lot longer to get to the take-off point. You have to queue, then travel up the mountain and get your kit on.'

'I'm prepared for that. I just think it will be such a great experience to paraglide down the mountain and on to the grass,'

Skiing went well, but as Anna predicted, they finished early in the afternoon. David enjoyed paragliding, eventually. The waiting about was tiresome and he wondered if he had made the right decision.

'I was very nervous as we pushed off from the top,' he said. 'I tried not to think too much about my predicament, with a harness holding me on to a strange-looking parachute. As we drifted around in the sky I appreciated the peace and beauty of it all and my nerves disappeared. At least my guide made an easy descent, not like some of them I saw, twisting and turning, backwards and forwards. Having floated gently down, I wondered what the landing would be like. I should have had no worries. It was as peaceful as the rest of the flight. The guide did all the work and we touched down without a hitch. Here I am to prove it.'

'You looked great as you came down,' said Anna, 'and really relaxed. I can't imagine me having a go at paragliding,' she said, 'I like my feet to be on solid ground.'

14

Bond, James Bond

Although much of the heavy midweek snowfall remained, the roads had been cleared sufficiently to make car travel less hazardous. However, David and Anna wouldn't be going by car. When she gave him more details of their Swiss holiday, she did point out that Mürren was a car-free resort. David had been in touch with the company who rented out the apartments where they would be staying in Grindelwald and he got permission to continue to park his car there while they would be in Mürren.

'The train journey from Grindelwald via Lauterbrunnen to Mürren is good, with more spectacular scenery,' said David. 'The reason I said we need only a medium case each, plus a large handbag for you and a shoulder bag for me, is because we have to carry these from the apartment in Grindelwald to the hotel in Mürren. I know most of the journey is on a train, but we still have to get the luggage on and off the train.'

Anna considered the weather cold enough to warrant wearing a fur hat, scarf and gloves. David thought she was overdressed compared with what he was wearing. His description of the scenery was spot on. The walk to the hotel was mainly uphill and when they eventually arrived and stood in front of it, they commented how large and impressive it looked. It was good to feel the warmth as they entered reception.

'Welcome,' said the receptionist, a tall serious-looking man wearing glasses and dressed in a dark suit. 'What are your names?'

'I am Anna Mustermann and this is Mr David Burrows, my partner.'

'Would you each please fill in your details on one of these forms? May I remind you there is a lockable safe in your room and you are advised to keep all your valuables in there? Breakfast each morning is from 0700.'

Having completed and signed the forms, Anna and David were given the keys to their room. The receptionist wished them a safe and enjoyable stay. They picked up their luggage and walked upstairs. After a quick freshen-up and drink, David and Anna emerged from the hotel well-wrapped against the chilly conditions.

'I have to admit Mürren is not a place I've visited before,' said Anna. 'From what we've seen so far it has a good selection of hotels,' she continued. Anna looked back to see David a few paces behind her. 'Come on old man! You'll never stand a chance of playing the part of James Bond if you can't walk, let alone ski!'

'OK! It's only supposed to be a gentle amble and there you are striding out in front!'

On a clear day there would have been many photo opportunities, but the mist which clung to the mountains and trees ruled them out today. After some good exercise David and Anna returned to the hotel, to have a shower and prepare themselves for the evening meal.

'How about doing a circular trip by train, cable car, and ski lift tomorrow?' David asked.

'That sounds like a good idea. And I know you want to go up Schilthorn, so you can pretend to be James Bond. Should we do that on Monday?'

'Right then, I had better start practising! Which Bond girl am I going to sleep with tonight?'

'There's only me,' replied Anna, 'so you don't get a lot of choice!'

'I can't be too fussy then, I'll just have to take what's available!'

When they went down for a meal that evening there was an older couple sitting on their own, with empty seats at their table. They looked like the quintessential older English couple on holiday, both in tweed suits, him with a plain tie and her with a pearl brooch. David associated the perfume she was wearing with that worn by older ladies.

'May we come and join you?' asked Anna.

'Please do,' said the man, who introduced himself as Kenneth and his wife as Virginia.

'We're David and Anna,' he said, leaving the older couple to assume they were married.

'You're here for the skiing I suppose,' said Kenneth. 'That's far beyond us now. We're here for a break and the fresh air. We come here every year.'

'What do you do when you're not on holiday in Mürren?' asked David.

'I own and manage an engineering business in the West Midlands,' came the reply.

Just then the waiter arrived to take Anna and David's orders. Virginia didn't look like a working wife. Anna tried to draw her into conversation by asking her questions, but it was hard going. Virginia painted a picture of herself as a wife who had never worked since she had been married. She looked after the house and made sure Kenneth's meals were ready at the right time. Even so, she had a cleaner who came in one day a week. She went out to shop once a week and made the occasional visit to the WI, but she found the others in that group a tiresome lot.

By the end of this particular conversation Anna had come to feel sorry for Virginia. However, she came over as someone who wasn't easily satisfied and had several moans to Anna in the few minutes they had been talking together.

David, on the other hand, had got on famously with Kenneth, who was an extrovert character and was keen to sing his own praises. He had weathered the storms during the lean years and had done well during the good times. David kept trying to rack his brain about the story he had heard concerning someone who had run a small engineering factory in the West Midlands. By the end of the meal it had dawned on David where that story had come from. It was John, his brother-in-law, who had talked about Emma's father, Karl, running an engineering firm in the West Midlands from 1960's till his death in the late 1980's. David thought it was too soon to start firing off questions to Kenneth about the company he owned and any possible links there may be with David's German father-in-law. These could be ways to start conversation the next time they met. Discussions continued throughout the meal, with the two men talking together and the two ladies separately. This was not how David and Anna would have liked it, but this was the way it happened. At no time did Kenneth and Virginia speak to each other, or involve themselves in each other's conversations.

'That was quite a bizarre discussion over our meal,' David said. 'Kenneth has done quite well for himself through the engineering company he owns, but he seems to have very little in the way of a relationship with his wife.'

'She, on the other hand, seems to spend her time providing for him and she rarely goes out,' Anna added. 'I did find out they have no children and they're both well beyond retiring age. When I asked her what will happen to the business in the future, Virginia looked up to the ceiling and said, "I don't know". By her body language and facial expression I thought she was going to add, "And I don't care!"'

'An interesting couple,' David said. 'I do hope we get a chance to meet them again. That's enough about them,' he continued. 'Now let's concentrate on us!'

'You took the words out of my mouth,' Anna said. 'If you're going to emulate James Bond you had better get started!'

'OK!' said David.

The next day it was gloomy again and it seemed the sun would never break through. 'Don't be too pessimistic,' Anna said. 'The sun will appear when you least expect it.' And she was right.

At various points during their trip it was like passing through a winter wonderland. 'It really is so breathtaking,' said David. 'It's only the cold that will put me off. There are more than enough camera shots up here. I'm spoilt for choice.'

As they descended from the snowy kingdom, the mist once again engulfed the train they were travelling in. It was a joy to thaw out in reception and then enjoy a hot shower. There was no sign of Kenneth and Virginia in the restaurant that night, so David and Anna ate alone. David thought he was being rather bold in asking Anna if she knew about Schilthorn, when she had lived most of her life amongst mountains. There was no way of knowing if she was familiar with the link between Schilthorn and James Bond.

'Do you know how the buildings on the top of Schilthorn came about?' he enquired.

'I know there's a link with James Bond, but I don't know the full story,' she replied.

A small Swiss company planned to build the longest cable car line in Europe, from Stechelberg via Grindelwald, Mürren, and Birg to Schilthorn. The original budget was 8.5 million Swiss Francs and construction began in 1961. The first three stages were completed by 1965 and became operational. By then the cost had soared to 25 million Swiss Francs, but with a further loan the project was completed and started running in 1967.'

'What has this to do with James Bond?' asked Anna.

'The production manager for the future James Bond movie, "On Her Majesty's Secret Service" saw the unfinished restaurant at the top of Schilthorn and thought it would be ideal as a location for the major part of the film, with the beautiful scenery and steep slopes ideal for the snow chases. The film production team completed the construction of the revolving restaurant, called Piz Gloria in the film, and brought in electricity for shooting the film. After filming was completed in March 1969, the company that had built the cable car line owed nothing for finishing the restaurant and the other structures in exchange for the rights to film on the premises. "On Her Majesty's Secret Service" was released in 1969 and grossed around 80 million US dollars.'

'And is that the reason you want to spend tomorrow on Schilthorn?'

'Yes. Most British men and boys feel an affinity with James Bond. They would all want to swap places with him.'

'Be honest, that's because of the women he attracts,' said Anna with more than a touch of sarcasm.

'I don't care what you say, I'm going to enjoy tomorrow!' David said, hoping to bring closure to this particular topic of conversation.

Hardly a word was spoken during breakfast. David always felt tense and uneasy before taking a trip be it by plane or cable car and he never wanted much to eat.

As he and Anna pushed their way into the cable car he remarked what a dangerous journey this would be, hanging from a piece of wire over a precipice. 'Don't be so silly,' Anna told him. 'How many times has this gone backwards and forwards between Mürren and Birg for over fifty years?'

Despite Anna's assurances David felt safer when he was out of the cable car. The second stage was better. He was full of admiration for the engineer who designed the ride that took the cable car within what looked like a few centimetres of the rock face as it docked.

'Let me get outside for a breath of fresh air,' David said.

'You'll certainly get plenty of that up here!' said Anna with a laugh.

David led the way to the viewing platform and marvelled at the spectacular panoramic view.

'Photos don't give a fair reflection, but they will remind me of what I've seen,' he said.

After that it was time for coffee and then a visit to the World of James Bond, complete with helicopter.

'I must have a go at the simulator,' David said. 'Are you coming?'

'No,' replied Anna. 'I'll just watch you.'

David was like a child at Christmas, having just opened his first high-tech toy. Anna then joined him to browse the James Bond exhibition.

'Something I don't understand,' said Anna. 'It says that "On Her Majesty's Secret Service" starred George Lazenby. I thought Sean Connery was James Bond.'

'He was, up till this time, but then George Lazenby played 007, for this film only.'

By the end of the morning David and Anna felt they had overdosed on 007 and they were in need of something to eat and drink. They went to the Piz Gloria revolving restaurant for sustenance and to chill out amongst the wonderful scenery.

'Here we can literally watch the world go round,' David joked.

As they dined, they could hear the sound of a helicopter flying around the Piz Gloria. 'Do you think they're making another film?' asked Anna.

'Probably not. Anyone can take a pleasure flight if they've got lots of money and don't mind skimming close to the mountain. I think the helicopter also picks up and drops off skiers. I'll investigate after we've eaten. I want to go and view the outside displays about James Bond too.'

A short time later there was the sound of an approaching helicopter and the constant loud sound as it came in to land. Then all was quiet for a while. David got up and started to walk towards the helicopter. 'I'm going to see what's happening', he said.

'How long will you be?' asked Anna.

'About 30 minutes,' David replied. 'If you go down to the terrace we can meet there.'

As David made his way down, he could see a helicopter parked on the snow. Two men walked across the snow towards it and the one dressed in white had a rifle slung over his shoulder. As soon as they climbed on board, the rotor blades started to turn slowly. The blades rotated more quickly and the noise became deafening. As the helicopter took off its blades flung swirls of powdery snow into the air and obscured it from David's view. He immediately rushed up on to the terrace to get a better view. As it turned and approached David he heard the unmistakeable sound of rifle shots echoing around the terrace. He hid behind one of the James Bond placards until the helicopter moved away. Then David ran to get a lift on the cable car, together with a crowd of others who were going down the mountain. As soon as he was able he phoned Anna and left a message, 'Go back down, D.' David assumed Anna had received the voicemail as there was nothing to say it couldn't be delivered. When the cable car reached Birg he raced to get into the one going down to Mürren. All this time his heart was pounding and he felt sick with worry. On arriving at Mürren David stood aside to let the rest of the passengers pass. As he stood there waiting, looking for Anna's face in the crowd, his mind went back a few hours to when he and Anna had been standing there holding hands as they waited to catch the cable car that would take them up to Schilthorn. Slowly the number of people going past him reduced, until the flow stopped altogether.

David was full of questions, but he had no idea where he would find any answers. Where was Anna? Was she still at Schilthorn, unable to get into the cable car he caught? Had she stopped at Birg and waited for him there? Was she at the front of the crowd that got off at Mürren? If so, where was she now?

David walked down to the road to see if Anna was there. He paused and dialled her mobile. All he got was a recorded message, 'The person you are calling is unable to take your call. Please leave your message after the tone.' He replied immediately, 'Hi darling, it's me. Where are you? I'm terribly worried about you. Please get in touch.'

David took a walk back to the empty cable car, but apart from members of staff, there was nobody else around. He went over and spoke to a man in uniform, 'Have you seen a lady waiting here?' he asked. 'She was wearing a blue coat and a red woolly hat. We got separated at the top. I came down on that last cable car, but when everybody else got off she was nowhere to be seen.' The man shook his head and said, 'Nein.'

'Danke,' replied David, as he walked in the direction of the road again. The only other possibility he could think of was that Anna had gone back to the hotel. There seemed to be no reason why she should have done that, but if she wasn't there, he could make enquiries at reception and register the fact that Anna had gone missing. The stern-looking receptionist was on duty; he always seemed to be on duty!

'Anna and I got separated from each other on Schilthorn and I have not been able to find her,' said David. 'I wonder if you have seen her. She was wearing a blue coat and a red woolly hat.'

'I can remember her leaving this morning and I thought how nice she looked. I haven't seen her since.'

'Would you let me have my room key, please? I'll see if I can find any clues there about what might have happened to her.'

'She hasn't been back here to collect the room key this afternoon,' said the receptionist, confirming his previous statement. He took the key from its hook and put it on the counter.

David walked hurriedly upstairs and opened the door. At first glance everything looked as it had been left earlier in the day. On closer inspection there was nothing that gave him cause for concern. He went back to reception and handed back the key saying, 'I really don't know where to go from here.'

'One thing you should do as soon as possible is to inform the police what has happened. They will come here and write down the details. I can telephone them and ask that they come to the hotel.'

'Thank you,' said David, 'I would appreciate that. Perhaps I can have my key again, so I can wait in my room for the police to arrive.' It was several minutes later when the phone rang and the receptionist announced that the police had arrived. David entered reception just as the receptionist was lifting the bar counter and ushering the two police officers into the room behind the bar.

'Ah, Mr Burrows,' he said, gesturing David to follow them. The room was quite small and contained various pieces of hotel equipment that looked as if they hadn't been used for years. There was sufficient space for the chairs, but it was a rather cosy arrangement! The two officers sat together. One was a tall, well-built young man and the other a diminutive lady. They both spoke English with a foreign accent and David found this easy to understand. The lady spoke first.

'What is your name?'

'David Burrows.'

'You live in England?'

'Originally, but now I live in Stuttgart.'

'What is your job?'

'I am Finance Director for the Mustermann Corporation, a large international organisation,' David said.

The male officer took up the questioning, 'Could I see you passport?'

David felt in his pockets. He immediately realised where it was. 'I don't seem to have it. I think it is in my partner's handbag,' David again fumbled in his pocket and took out his ID card. 'I do have this,' he said and handed it to the officer, who scrutinised it and made notes on his pad.

He turned to look at David and said, 'Tell me, Mr Burrows, what happened to you today.' As he listened, he continued to look intently at David.

'My partner and I spent the day on Schilthorn. After lunch I left her in the Piz Gloria restaurant and I went to take a look at the James Bond exhibition and everything to do with the making of the film, "On Her Majesty's Secret Service". As I came outside again, there was a helicopter flying around the Piz Gloria Restaurant. As it banked, it threw snow into the air, so for a few seconds it was difficult to see anything. Then I heard rifle shots and I ran for cover. I rang Anna, my partner, telling her to go back down in the cable car. At that time there seemed to be a lot of people trying to go down from Schilthorn.'

'Let me stop you there,' said the officer. 'You said you heard shots. Did you see anyone with a gun?'

'Yes,' said David, 'and I could hear bullets ricocheting off the objects on the terrace.'

'So you rang Anna, telling her to go down in the cable car. Do you know if she received your call?'

'I think so. There was no message to make me think otherwise,' David said.

'Do you think there was a real gunman firing bullets, or could it have been someone, somewhere, firing dummy bullets to demonstrate how a scene in the film was made?'

'I thought they were real bullets,' said David, trying to convince the officer that someone had been firing at him.

The police officer then asked about the cable car trip down. 'As people were crowding into the cable car to go down the mountain, did they appear to be fleeing in panic from a gunman, or was there a crowd because so many people wanted to go down at the same time?'

'I was fleeing from a gunman,' David said. 'I assumed everybody else was doing the same.'

'But you can't be sure why the rest of the crowd was all going down at the same time?'

'No,' replied David.

'What happened next?'

'We got down to Birg. There was no sign of Anna waiting for me there. I managed to catch the next train down to Mürren. At this stage I had no idea if Anna was in the same cable car as me, or if she was ahead or behind me. When we arrived at Mürren, I allowed everyone else to go past me. When the cable car was empty, I asked a member of staff if he had seen anyone fitting the description of Anna, wearing a blue coat and a red hat.'

'What did he say?'

'No, he hadn't. I then walked slowly back to the hotel and told the receptionist. He said he would phone the police and you arrived soon afterwards.'

The police officer finished making notes. He shook his head as he looked towards David.

'This is a terrible event that has taken place. You have no idea where Anna could have gone?' David shook his head. 'Could she have met up with some friends?'

'No,' said David. 'We were staying in Mürren for a week on our own.'

The police officer ran the fingers of his left hand over his chin as he thought deeply about what he had heard. After several minutes he looked at David and said, 'I would like you to accompany us to our police headquarters, so we can question you further.'

'But I've told you all I know,' said David plaintively.

'Yes, but we have other interrogators there who can perhaps pick up on something I have missed. See this whole episode from my point of view. Two people spend a day on a mountain and only one of them returns. Who could be responsible for the disappearance of the one who fails to come back? The one who did return, of course! I need to question you more, to eliminate you from my enquiry, or to gain sufficient evidence to convict you. With nothing else to go on at present, Mr Burrows, you are my number one suspect!'

15

Lost

David was taken by car to the police headquarters and shown into a room that was more suitable as a place for conducting interviews than was the storeroom at the hotel. He was driven there by Police Officer Egger, who had conducted much of the first interview and was now in charge of this subsequent interrogation. The female police officer had been replaced by an older gentleman in plain clothes. He wouldn't have looked out of place as a senior fellow at a university or serving on the board of directors for a large corporation. When he spoke there was a slight hint of a German accent and his deep voice was both gentle and reassuring.

'I have been briefed about the sudden disappearance of Anna Mustermann earlier today,' he said looking at his notes. Then he removed his glasses, and after putting them on the table, he continued in the same sonorous tone. 'There are a number of things that could have happened to Anna. Firstly, she could have wandered off on her own, or forgotten where she had arranged to meet you,' he said, looking at David. 'In her lost state one of two things may have befallen her. She could have had an accident and fallen to her death, or she could have suffered a health problem, such as a stroke or heart attack, or a mental aberration such as amnesia. Once I have completed my list of possibilities as to what may have happened to Anna, I will ask for your thoughts, Mr Burrows.'

David's mind had been in a whirl since he became aware that Anna was missing, but the clear and concise words of the eminent practitioner had opened up avenues for consideration that he hadn't previously thought of.

Doctor Buchman, whose name David only learned towards the end of the interview, went on, 'Other explanations for Anna's disappearance may involve a third party. In other words, she may have been kidnapped or killed. In this eventuality, who would have kidnapped her? Who might have killed her? Who would want to see her dead?

David thanked Doctor Buchman for his eloquent description of the possibilities by which Anna may have disappeared. He thought some background information would not come amiss. 'Anna and I were just into the second week of an excellent holiday in Switzerland; the first week in Grindelwald and now the second week in Mürren. I have to say there have been a few strange things happen since we left Stuttgart.'

'Tell me,' said the doctor.

'On the Autobahn as we travelled here we had a car full of young people making gestures and shouting at us.'

'What sort of car was it?'

'A blue Subaru,' David said. 'Then, when we were on one of the ski slopes two marshals spent a lot of time looking at me through binoculars.'

'Did they come and speak to you?'

'No,' replied David, 'but I felt I was being carefully watched.'

Police Officer Egger then asked a question. 'Is there anything else you want to tell us about?' he said.

'When we were coming down on the Jungfrau Express we could see skiers carrying rifles, going in the same direction as the train. Anna had an explanation for this, but seeing them skiing alongside the train made me feel uneasy. Undoubtedly the worst experience was on Schilthorn today. A helicopter flew low around Piz Gloria and blew snow into the air. For a few seconds I couldn't see anything and during that time I could hear rifle shots on the terrace where I was standing. I'm convinced someone was shooting at me.'

'Who would want to kill you?' asked the Police Officer.

'I don't know,' replied David, 'but I definitely felt under attack.'

'And you can't think of anyone who would like to see Anna dead?'

'No, not at all!'

'What about people from her past, business associates, previous partners, or even so-called friends?'

'I have known Anna for less than two years, so my knowledge of her previous relationships is severely limited,' David said.

Police Officer Egger continued, 'As I consider what might have happened to Anna, as described by Doctor Buchman, there has been no report of any body being found, so this seems to rule out an accident, heart attack or stroke. We will continue to follow up any information concerning possible kidnap or murder, but so far we have no leads to investigate further. I ask that you surrender your ID card and you remain at the hotel for the next few days.'

'I am happy to cooperate with the police as fully as I can, until I discover the fate of my dear Anna,' said David. 'I will continue to stay in the hotel till the end of the week.' With that David gave in his ID card, shook hands with the police officer and Doctor Buchman and left the police headquarters.

As soon as David arrived back at the hotel he telephoned Sue, to let her know what had happened. 'Sue, I've got some terrible news to pass on. Anna has gone missing!'

'What? How? I can't believe that,' his daughter said.

'We were on the top of Schilthorn, where one of the James Bond films was made. I went outside to look at some of the displays about the film. A helicopter swooped low, sending snow into the air and then I heard shots being fired.'

'Did Anna get shot?'

'No, I don't think so. I can't be sure what happened after that. I rang her mobile and told her to go down in the cable car. When I got down I couldn't find her! Did she get lost at the top and fail to make her way down? Did she fall prey to an individual or group of people? Where is she now? Is she still alive?'

'Oh Daddy! I don't know what to say. I'm so far away I can't do anything. You two made such a good couple. She was an ideal companion for you after Mummy died.'

'I'm beside myself with worry,' David said. 'I'll give Steve a call next. I've been interviewed by the police. At first I was treated as the chief suspect, but I get the feeling I've been moved down the list after the second interview tonight. Anna has, or had, my passport. I've just had to hand in my ID card and I must stay at the hotel for the next few days.'

'Tell us how we can help,' said Sue. 'Keep in touch and do let us know any news.'

The telephone conversation with Steve followed a similar pattern. 'Hi Steve, it's Dad. Anna has somehow got lost while we were on the top of a mountain. We were in two different places. A helicopter was flying around and I heard rifle shots.'

'What a nightmare!' Steve exclaimed. 'Was Anna actually shot dead?'

'I don't think so. No body has been found. When I got down from the mountain I couldn't find Anna. I've been interviewed by the police and told to stay in the hotel till the end of the week.'

'How dreadful!' Steve said. 'As soon as you can, you need to get yourself back to the UK, where Sue and Tom, Jo and I can support you. We need to work out a plan about what you might do.'

'At the moment I just don't know which way to turn and where to start looking for Anna. I'll keep you in touch with developments.' With that David rang off, feeling absolutely bereft.

After making his phone calls David needed a stiff drink, so he hurried down to the bar. The place was empty apart from the barman clearing up. He ordered a double whisky, which he drank at top speed, hoping it would drown his sorrows. David knew he wouldn't sleep very well, but he hoped the whisky would at least help to heal his heartache.

The next day David spent most of the morning in his room, but he ventured down to the restaurant for lunch. He picked up a local paper and skimmed through it for any news of a missing female holidaymaker. His German was sufficiently proficient to glance at the various stories and articles and know there was nothing related to Anna's disappearance.

Kenneth and Virginia came in and joined him for lunch. They were surprised Anna was not with him. David explained what had happened the previous day.

'What a terrible tragedy,' said Kenneth. 'She was such a pretty young thing.'

Virginia even got herself involved in the conversation, expressing heartfelt sympathy to David. 'What a sad thing to happen in the middle of your holiday,' she said.

'At what time did Anna go missing?' asked Kenneth.

'Sometime in the middle of the afternoon,' replied David.

'And was that when you came down from Schilthorn and realised she wasn't in the cable car?'

'Yes,' David said. 'I expected her to be somewhere in the crowd. It was only when everyone had left the cable car that I knew she wasn't with me.'

'Do you remember when we went for a stroll yesterday afternoon?' Kenneth asked Virginia, holding her arm as if to get her attention and remind her of what happened. 'There was a blue car parked in the distance,' he went on. 'As we continued to walk, a lady got into the car and it drove off. My eyes are not as good as they used to be and I didn't recognise her, but could that have been Anna?' he asked.

'Did you see anyone else?' David asked. 'You seem to imply that the lady got into the car willingly. She wasn't forced to get in?'

'No. She got in on her own.' said Kenneth.

'That would mean she wasn't kidnapped, or taken for a ransom,' said David. 'I must let the police know what you have just told me.'

Virginia, who hadn't been involved in this recent conversation concerning a lady and a blue car, wanted to know more about David and Anna. 'Have you been married long?' she enquired.

'We're not actually married, said David. 'I have known Anna for the past eighteen months. Our love for each other has been growing since we first met.'

'Such a pity Anna has gone missing now,' Virginia added.

David ignored this change in direction of the conversation and turned to speak with Kenneth. 'I remember you saying the other day that you purchased an engineering business in the West Midlands. Do you happen to know the name of the person from whom you bought the company?'

'I'm sorry, I don't. It was all done through an agent. Why do you ask?' said Kenneth.

'I knew someone who sold an engineering firm in the West Midlands around the same time. I thought it would be a coincidence if it had been the same person; that was all.'

The conversation continued for sometime, with Kenneth and Virginia putting forward further ideas to explain how Anna had disappeared. Having finished his lunch David took his leave from the elderly couple, saying he would go and give the police a ring about the information Kenneth had told him. He said he hoped he would meet up with them again before they all left Mürren.

When David rang the police headquarters the duty officer told him that neither of the officers he had spoken with previously was available. He left a message for one of them to return his call as soon as possible. At the end of the afternoon Police Officer Egger telephoned him.

'I believe you have some information for me, Mr Burrows,' the officer said.

'At lunchtime in the hotel I had a meal with an elderly couple from England. The man said there had been a blue car parked some distance away from them while they were having a stroll yesterday afternoon. At some point a young lady answering Anna's description got into the car and was driven away. Kenneth, the witness, did say he suffers from poor vision, but this sighting may give you something to go on.'

'For every case that is investigated there are literally thousands of pieces of evidence to follow up,' said the officer. 'Many of these have no relevance at all. However, any evidence may help me to build up a bigger picture of what happened yesterday afternoon. I will go and visit the hotel and take a statement from the gentleman, whose name is Kenneth.'

'I'm sorry I don't know his second name.'

'No worry. Thank you for passing on this information, Mr Burrows.'

David then telephoned Klaus and Franz; a call he was not looking forward to making. Klaus answered and David briefly described what happened. 'Yesterday afternoon as Anna and I were coming down from Schilthorn, we got separated. When I reached the cable car stop in Mürren there was no sign of Anna. After searching for a while I went back to the hotel and the receptionist reported the matter to the police for me.'

'I am sorry to hear that you have lost Anna,' Klaus said in a voice that sounded as though he was trying to suppress a laugh. 'This is most unfortunate. Have the police made any progress in finding her?'

'So far there is no trace of Anna and I have no idea what might have happened. I thought I should let you know and I will keep you informed of any developments,' David said, ending the conversation and leaving no opportunity for further taunts from his boss. One thing Klaus' words had done was to indicate the seriousness of the situation by describing Anna as lost. This had the effect of taking David back to his childhood and bringing him into the present in quick succession.

Once David was on holiday with his family at the seaside. He was about ten at the time. He went off to get himself an ice-cream, but failed to return. His father and mother were beside themselves with worry. His father went and spoke to the life guards about David's disappearance and reported the matter to the police. It was two hours before a policeman returned him to his parents. David had bought and eaten an ice-cream, but then lost his bearings. He could still remember the sense of loneliness and isolation as though it happened only yesterday.

Back in the present, David accepted that Anna was missing, but a new revelation emerged; he was lost without Anna. She was what had kept him going since Emma had died. She was the reason he now lived in Germany and worked for the Mustermann Corporation.

She was his inspiration and soul-mate. What would he do without her? He hardly dare contemplate the possibility. He must push on and do everything he could to find Anna.

That night David had a dream that he was walking through a forest and everything was in black, white, or grey. The tree trunks were black or grey, but as soon as he shone his torch on them they turned white. It was an eerie experience walking amongst the trees and from the depths of the forest he could hear muffled voices calling out, 'Where is Emma? Have you lost her? You must keep looking!' As time went on David became more anxious and he broke out in a cold sweat. At various times in his life he had lost his mother, father, and Emma; and now Anna. This thought cast an ugly shadow over the trees and turned the white trunks to grey or black. When he awoke he felt he had done battle with alien forces that had left him completely drained.

During the next few days there was no more news about Anna's disappearance. David took the initiative and phoned the police headquarters, only to be told that there were no further developments. He then phoned his children to pass on this information. 'I will travel back to Stuttgart on Saturday,' David said, 'so I can sort out anything that needs to be done at work. Then I will travel to the UK early next week.'

'I'm glad you said that,' Sue replied. 'I suggest we all meet up at the cottage next weekend, to plan what we're going to do with you.'

'You make me sound like a rebellious teenager, or a dog that needs taking in hand,' said David.

Sue gave a chuckle. 'You know what I mean,' she added.

Steve, too, thought it was a good idea for David to travel back to England and for the family to meet up to make decisions about his father's future.

Kenneth and Virginia checked out of the hotel on Friday morning. 'It's quite a journey when you're our age,' said Kenneth. 'It will give us the weekend to recover before we start a new week.'

'I do hope you will have better news about dear Anna soon,' said Virginia. She handed David a crumpled piece of paper. 'Do give us a ring whenever you hear any news.'

David arranged with the police officer to collect his ID card on Saturday morning. Then he had to steel himself to carry two cases and his shoulder bag to Grindelwald on the train. Thankfully the car trip back to Stuttgart was uneventful. On Sunday he chilled out and planned to go in to work to meet Klaus and Franz on Monday.

'Klaus and I are very sorry to hear that Anna has gone missing,' said Franz, as David walked into the main office. 'We offer you our heartfelt sympathy. We could, of course, put forward all sorts of ideas and explanations as to how Anna disappeared, but they would be guesses. We must leave the police to do their job. We hope Anna will be found alive and well very soon. I'm sure she will.'

David thanked Franz for his kind words. 'At the moment I am in complete shock over what has happened,' he said. 'With your permission,' David continued, looking first at Klaus and then at Franz, 'I would like to go back to the UK, to try and sort out what I might do in the future.'

'We quite understand,' said Franz, 'but you seem to have adopted a pessimistic outlook and you already assume that Anna is dead. Within a few days Anna might turn up somewhere and all the doom and gloom will be forgotten.'

'Perhaps I am expecting the worst possible outcome,' continued David, 'and someone will find Anna's body, or she never reappears. I need to have some plan in place for my future whatever the eventuality. As you will appreciate, I'm here because of Anna. I couldn't contemplate being here without her. I wouldn't be able to go on working for the Mustermann Corporation. I would want to return to the UK and live and work there.'

'I think we would expect that,' said Franz. 'However, you do still have some assignments to be done and when these are completed; we would be willing to terminate your contract. This can be negotiated at a later date. In the meantime let's be positive and expect Anna to come back within the next few days.'

David thanked Franz and Klaus for their understanding and support. 'If this is convenient,' he said, 'I will leave tomorrow to go back to the UK. I am hoping to have regular contact with you and the Swiss police.'

'We are in complete agreement with these plans,' Franz said. Both he and Klaus moved forward to shake hands with David as he stood up to leave.

16

Home

David had phoned Pat a few days earlier to let her know he would be returning to the UK for an indefinite period. As he sat in the lounge surveying all that was familiar, his mind went back to the first few years when he and Emma lived in the cottage. It looked so different then, inside and out. When they first arrived there were a number of jobs to be done, to make the house weatherproof and as comfortable as possible. Threadbare patches of carpet were covered with cheap rugs bought in Tonbridge. This was an ideal place to bring up two young children, who frequently invited their friends round to play. It didn't matter that food and all manner of liquids got spilt on the floors. The carpets were replaced when the children were out of nappies.

The garden was so overgrown with nettles and brambles that David had to enlist the help of a contractor to remove them before he could embark on his ambitious plan to create a new garden layout. A few trees and shrubs remained as the foundation for David's garden design project. It was great to have such wide open spaces where the children could play in safety.

David remembered the fun he, Emma and the children had in the house playing games like Murder in the Dark and Sardines. It was good when Sue and Steve had birthdays and invited their friends round to have tea. It was especially exciting when there were just the four of them and he and Emma would let their hair down and they became like kids again. These occasions showed the children that Mummy and Daddy were not always serious and boring.

Emma took on the rough and tumble of motherhood during those early years. It was not uncommon for David to come home and find Emma at her wits end as a result of looking after the children all day. As soon as he arrived home and helped to put the children to bed with a story, Emma revived with the help of a glass of wine. It was only when she returned to work and became Health Centre Manager that she took on a more serious attitude to life and she began to behave in a way that demonstrated she thought playing games was beneath her dignity. David on the other hand was always prepared to join in and have a laugh!

David was keen on the outdoor life and encouraged the rest of the family to be involved. When the children were getting towards the end of their time at Junior School the Burrows family would go away for the occasional weekend to experience the great outdoors under canvas. Before the first trip away David suggested they try a taster session in the back garden, to see how well they took to it. Emma was not convinced, but Sue and Steve persuaded her with the promise of a proper toilet and shower in the cottage and a real cooker in the kitchen. David did cook on an impromptu barbecue to make the experience as realistic as possible. After a few years they had spent a number of weeks in such idyllic settings as the Lake District, the Peak District and the North York Moors.

As David now strolled around his garden, memories continued to fill his mind. He remembered the time that Sue fell off her bike and grazed her knee on the gravel drive. She shrieked and cried for a long time and it took all David's fatherly care and sympathy to make it better. One morning at breakfast Steve boasted that he had a wiggly tooth. He should have remained quiet! Later one of his friends helped to remove it with a classic cover drive that caught Steve full in the mouth. The tooth was found beneath a splendid elm which grew where David was now standing, its life cut short by Dutch elm disease. Steve took the injury in his stride and the tooth was put out for the tooth fairy that night!

After indulging himself in fond memories David moved indoors to make himself a cup of tea. His search of the cupboards was rewarded when he discovered some biscuits and fruit cake, recently put there by Pat. She knew he was fond of fruitcake and thought it would make him feel particularly welcome back to the cottage. As he was finishing the last crumbs, the doorbell rang.

He wondered who it might be, bearing in mind few people knew he was back in the UK. As he opened the door Pat's smiling face greeted him.

'How good to see you. Come on in,' he said, giving her a peck on the cheek. 'Where's Tony?'

'He's taken advantage of the better weather to get out in the garden,' Pat replied, as they walked arm in arm down the hall.

'I've just made myself a cup of tea, to go with that splendid fruitcake. I'd appreciate it if you'd join me. Is that OK? Fine! I'll make a fresh pot,' David said, putting fresh cups and saucers, milk and sugar on a tray, while Pat watched. Having made the tea he added the teapot to the tray.

'I thought you might appreciate a visit,' she went on. 'One thing I'm intrigued to know is why have you come back home? I guess Anna couldn't get time off to come with you.'

'I'll explain that in a minute,' he said, picking up the tray and leading the way into the lounge. He realised the next few minutes were not going to be easy.

'Anna and I were enjoying a wonderful holiday in Switzerland. About a week ago we spent a day on the mountain where 'On Her Majesty's Secret Service' was filmed. I went out on the terrace to look at stills from the film and information boards about how the film was made. A helicopter was flying around the terrace and suddenly I heard gunshots. I took cover as I thought someone was trying to kill me. I rang Anna and left a message telling her to go down on the cable car.

I expected to see her at the last stop, but when I arrived, she wasn't there.'

'How terrible!' said Pat. 'What did you do?'

'I searched for her over several minutes. Every time another cable car descended I made a careful search of the passengers, but she wasn't amongst them. I then walked back to the hotel. She wasn't there either. The receptionist phoned the police for me. At first I was the main suspect, but since then I've been helping the police with their enquiries and they no longer consider me a suspect.' David paused to drink some tea.

'What could have happened to Anna? Have the police come up with any ideas?' asked Pat.

'Any possible explanations about what might have happened have nothing to substantiate them,' David said. 'She may have suffered an accident, but no body has been found. She may have been kidnapped, but by whom? Nobody has come forward to say they saw Anna being bundled into a car. She may have wandered off and got lost, but there have been no reported sightings of Anna. The only possible lead comes from an elderly couple out for a stroll in Mürren the afternoon Anna disappeared. They watched from a distance as a woman got into a blue car, but the man did say his eyesight is failing. No other witnesses have come forward with information about what happened.'

'This is all most distressing,' said Pat. 'Where does this leave you?'

'It leaves me feeling absolutely distraught. There is not a shred of evidence to indicate what might have happened. I am in limbo; my life has been put on hold,' he said, as he covered his face with his hands. 'I went and explained to my employers what had happened and I have been given compassionate leave. I don't know how long that will last. I don't want to work in Germany without Anna. If she fails to return, I won't be going back there. I realise I have some responsibilities to my employers. I work on an assignment basis. It's like being back at school! I need to complete some further assignments before I can be released from my contract.'

'What if the worst scenario happens and Anna fails to come back,' asked Pat.

'I certainly won't be working in Germany,' David replied.

'What will you do then?'

'There must be lots of employers looking for someone who's had experience in banking and finance, overseas trading and investment.'

'Possibly so,' said Pat, 'but someone in his early fifties? People of this age are the most difficult to employ. They expect high salaries, but are unlikely to stay long.'

'OK, I haven't started my quest yet, so maybe I'm being over-optimistic,' David said, bringing that particular topic of conversation to a close. He didn't want to get into a protracted argument with someone who had experience of working in HR and running an employment agency.

'At the moment I feel like a cat on a hot tin roof,' he said. 'I don't know what to sort out first. Assuming

Anna never returns I will cut my ties with Germany and return to the UK. Then one of my priorities must be to get myself a job, which you suggest is not going to be as easy as it sounds. I also need to get myself a social life, which is just as important to me as getting a job.'

'But although you've not been away long, things have changed and you can't expect to carry on where you left off!' Pat interjected.

'Perhaps I'm being over-optimistic in expecting to slot back in again quickly,' said David.

'I think you are,' said Pat, wrinkling up her nose. 'Relationships take time to develop and don't happen overnight.'

'But why change the habit of a lifetime?' As soon as he said it, David realised how inappropriate his comment had been. 'I'm sorry, I shouldn't have said that,' he added.

'That's you all over,' Pat said. 'You come out with some comment before you've thought about it and the impact your words will have. Like the time a number of couples went away together for a weekend. When we got back to Tonbridge, Emma went straight home. It was obvious to most of us that she'd had enough of your Jack the Lad behaviour and wanted a break. And what did you do? You looked to get off with another member of the opposite sex and I soon realised it was me you had your eyes on. That was so unfair! Emma wasn't there to take you in hand and suggest that you two should leave. Tony wouldn't say or do anything. He's not like that. Even if you turned up at our house with a coach and horses and walked me down our path, he still wouldn't get annoyed.'

'When was this?' David asked. 'I can't remember it!'

'It must have been ten years or more ago. We went to a music festival in Devon.'

'So how did I come on to you?'

'You'd had too much to drink and you were very touchy-feely. When I realised what was going on I suggested to Tony that we leave.'

'Oh yes! It was not unusual for Emma to get annoyed and go off in a huff.'

'Well you'd better be warned. You can't just come back here and take up with who you fancy.'

'Thanks for the warning!'

'It's time I was off,' Pat said looking at her watch. 'I've probably said too much anyway.'

'No! I've appreciated you coming round. I'm not so sure about the character assassination, but it will do me good to heed your wise words.'

Pat got up and left without looking back at David. She thought it would be a long time before she returned to the cottage when David was there alone. He had experienced quite a mauling and it was painful. He had always considered Pat as a very good friend to Emma during her troubles and to him and the family since her death. David considered Pat a person of integrity, but he felt her harsh criticism was out of all proportion.

'Ah well,' he said to himself, 'forewarned is forearmed!' He would have to watch his step in future.

The meeting with the family was altogether different. The adults were very supportive… Sue and Tom had told Rachel and James that somehow Anna had got lost and warned them not to ask Grandpa any questions. Over a meal that Sue and Jo had prepared, David outlined events on Schilthorn on the fateful day when Anna went missing.

'Have you heard anything from the Swiss police since you've been home,' Tom asked.

'Nothing at all,' replied David. 'There is one piece of information I can tell you. There was an old couple from the West Midlands staying in the same hotel as us in Mürren. Anna and I shared a table with them the night before Anna disappeared. As he said this he wiped away a tear with the back of his hand. 'They joined me for lunch the day after Anna went missing. When I told them what had happened, Kenneth, the man, told me what he had seen the previous afternoon. Apparently he and his wife were out for a walk and he noticed a blue car in the distance. After a while a lady got into the car and it drove off. Kenneth wondered if the lady could have been Anna. I passed on this information to the police, but I've had no phone calls about possible sightings of the blue car, or the lady who got into it. Kenneth did say his sight is fading, so I wonder how reliable a witness the police consider him.'

'There is one other snippet of information that may or may not be relevant,' David continued. 'On our way

235

driving along the Autobahn to Grindelwald, a blue Subaru came alongside us. The driver continually honked his horn and a number of young people were hanging out of the windows and making various gestures at us. I eventually managed to pull off the Autobahn and lose them. In Grindelwald there was a blue Subaru parked by the apartments where we were staying. While I was taking an early stroll one morning, a well-dressed man with a briefcase got into the Subaru and drove away. He didn't look the type to be associated with a bunch of unruly young people!'

David was keen to conclude the story of Anna going missing. He said, 'I think it's stretching credibility too far to suppose the Subaru on the Autobahn and/or the one parked in Grindelwald are in any way linked with the car Kenneth saw in Mürren and in which a lady resembling Anna was driven away. I don't think these incidents are connected.

'Can we now turn to another matter in which we as your family want to be closely involved?' said Sue. 'I'm talking about you getting another job.'

'We want to help and support you,' Steve said, 'but we're not sure what your intentions are.'

David outlined his thoughts. 'I think it's a simple choice. If Anna returns I stay in Germany and look for another job there.'

'The implication being that you wouldn't stay with the Mustermann Corporation,' said Steve.

'Yes! Things haven't been too good lately. If Anna doesn't come back I'll return to the UK and look for employment here.'

'What would you do?' asked Sue.

'Look for something in banking or finance,' David replied.

'But that may not be as easy as you think,' warned Tom.

'You see your age is against you,' added Steve.

'Have you been talking with Pat, Mum's friend?' asked David. 'She popped in to see me a few days ago and said exactly the same thing. I suppose I'm looking on the bright side. If Anna comes back I won't need a job in the UK.

'But if we are to be helpful and supportive, we need to know what's happening. You need to keep us up to date with what's going on,' said Sue.

'I'll do my best,' David replied, in a non-committal way. One thing I can say is that my will says that my estate, including the cottage, will be shared between Sue and Steve,' he said, looking at them in turn.

'This all sounds so morbid,' said Steve. 'We're not expecting you to die soon. You might outlive some of us.'

As days stretched into weeks and with no more news about Anna, David made up his mind to take the initiative for his life to have a pattern and purpose and be lived to the full. He began making a list of people he should visit and the things he should accomplish. Peter

Meadows had already asked him to have a round of golf, so he could ring him and agree a date. Now he had time on his hands he could ring Brian's wife and arrange to see her. Every time he telephoned there was no reply and no answering machine.

Having a drink in the Chafford Arms was high on David's list, so he drove there one night. There were new people in the bar and some of his former drinking friends were missing. As he launched into telling the story for the umpteenth time of how Anna went missing, he wished he could show a video and then just answer questions at the end. After telling the story, the questions began and kept coming thick and fast. David wasn't sure how well he was connecting with his audience. Some were new to Penshurst, others had moved on in their lives and for some, David's recent history was but a distant memory. After a while he began to feel like an outsider, unable to fit back into the area where he used to live. He overheard someone say, 'He's got what he wanted and now he'll have to live with the consequences!'

When he arrived home he felt a real sense of rejection. When Emma died at least he had Anna to help him build a new life. Now Anna had been lost from his life, there was no longer anybody there to help him pick up the pieces. He wanted to socialise, but things didn't work out. He felt more lonely than ever and realised he was on a downward spiral of depression and unable to do anything about it.

David had now reached the depths of loneliness and craved for female companionship, but Pat had warned him of the consequences of that course of action. I know what I'll do, he thought, I'll give Peter Meadows a ring and arrange to play golf with him over the next few days. David wasn't prepared for the shock he received when he spoke to Angela, Peter's wife. 'I'm sorry, David,' she said, 'I have to give you some very sad news. Peter died of a heart attack last week!'

He stayed silent for a couple of minutes and then came out with such a tirade of expletives that Angela had no other option but to put the phone down. David put his head in his hands and cried out loudly. 'What's happening to me, Dear God? My life seems to be falling apart!' He continued to howl like an injured dog. Peter hadn't been a close friend, but he was someone David had spoken to just a few days ago. Now he was dead! Was there no justice and comfort for a hurting soul? He stood up and took a bottle from the drinks cabinet and after pouring himself a large glass, he downed it in one. The first was followed by a second, then a third in quick succession. Soon he became uncontrollably drunk.

The next morning he woke up in a pool of vomit and tottered off to have a shower and a change of clothes. He flopped on to the bed and spent the early part of the day sleeping off his hangover. What would Emma have said if she had seen him in such a state? How would Anna have responded? He vowed never to allow himself to descend to such depths again. After all, he didn't sink so low when his two lovers had been taken from him. David resolved to spend as much time as possible fulfilling his dream of developing his garden into a thing of beauty that could be enjoyed by all who wished to visit it. This could be his legacy; the thing he would be remembered for into the future. The garden project occupied David's mind for weeks. He spent as much time outside as the weather would allow, transforming plans into reality. Flower beds and borders gradually took shape and he marvelled at what he had achieved, as plants came into flower.

In spite of everything, David was still a lonely, troubled man. He was uncertain to whom he could turn to get help in overcoming the attacks that assaulted his mind every day. What about Dr Brown? He had helped Emma, but would he be prepared to see David? Perhaps he was beginning to understand something of what Emma went through leading up to her death. The worst part was being unable to do anything to shake off the feelings of uselessness and low self esteem. The garden project had lifted David's spirit. Now all the negative thoughts and influences had pulled him back down again. He had never suffered from depression before, so he didn't know what the future held for him.

David's thoughts turned once more to what happened in Mürren several weeks ago. The time between then and now had contrived to draw a cloud over the whole episode. His mind was unlikely to come up with some brilliant ideas to explain exactly what happened on that day. The old adage 'No news is good news', certainly didn't hold true in this case. Since he travelled from Mürren and then on to the UK, he had heard absolutely nothing. What was good about that? Why hadn't someone been in contact to pass on some information about how Anna disappeared? He thought the police would have been in touch to verify something he had said. It was as if the police had lost his contact details. If that was Anna getting into the car, surely someone else must have seen her, in addition to Kenneth. David still believed Anna was alive, so there must be someone out there who knew of her whereabouts. Why is he or she not passing on details to the press or the police? In a moment of inspiration David's mind moved to the motive for her being abducted. Ransom demands are made soon after a person is kidnapped. However, what if a demand is made by email or mobile and for some reason the message hasn't got through? Perhaps a third party has intercepted the message and is waiting till the time is right to try a spot of blackmail. David wondered how much Klaus and Franz had been kept up to date with information on Anna. He had a hunch that they were better informed than he was. Would it have been better if he had stayed in Germany? One thing was for certain; spending time going over the possibilities in his mind had certainly moved Anna's disappearance to centre stage once more. He felt motivated to continue to come up with suggestions, knowing one of them was more-than-likely to be what actually happened!

17

Final Assignment

'Good Morning, Mr Burrows,' said Doctor Brown. 'I can't say I expected to see you as my first patient on a Monday morning, together with your daughter, Sue. How can I help?'

'Over the past few weeks I've been suffering from loss of memory,' said David. 'I can't remember people's names. Sometimes I start a sentence and I can't finish it.'

'We all suffer from those experiences as we get older. They're associated with the ageing process. It even happens to me, you'll be glad to know!' said the doctor. 'Is there something that could have triggered these memory lapses?'

'Yes,' said David. 'Anna, my partner, went missing some weeks ago. We were on holiday in Switzerland and she just disappeared. Nothing has been heard about her since. The matter has been reported to the Swiss police, but no trace of Anna has been found.'

'I'm sorry to hear Anna has disappeared. I think it's highly likely that her disappearance was such a traumatic event that your brain was thrown into shock and is taking time to adjust to the changing circumstances. Let me know about any changes, good or bad, that you experience in the next few days. I will make arrangements for you to have a memory test,' he said looking at David. He wrote on a card for him to attend on Wednesday at 9.00am. 'When we have the results, I can see if any medicine is required. In the meantime try to keep active, go out and meet people. Try to avoid staying at home and watching too much television.'

As the doctor concluded his advice he shook hands with David and Sue.

'Let's go and have a coffee,' she said. 'We need it after a session like that.'

'OK! Then you get off home; you've got plenty to do without having to worry about me,' David said.

'We're not desperately worried about you, but concerned. We want you to keep fit and healthy for as long as possible.'

'I do appreciate your concern. I thought the doctor was quite optimistic about my condition. The one thing that would change things dramatically would be if Anna appeared alive and well. I will give you and Doctor Brown an update when there is any change.'

David was becoming increasingly dissatisfied with the Swiss police. He still hadn't heard anything. He thought there would have been some news by now, one way or the other. He rang Police Officer Egger in Mürren and was surprised to be put in touch with him straight away.

'I apologise, Mr Burrows, that I have not been in contact with you, but I have absolutely nothing to report.'

'You must have received some fresh information about Anna going missing,' shouted David.

'I'm sorry, there hasn't been one single shred of new evidence,' the officer said.

David thought perhaps he should ask if there had been any exchange of information between Police Officer Egger and Klaus and Franz Mustermann, but he considered he was unlikely to receive an honest answer. However, the officer inadvertently answered David's unspoken question.

'I understand you will be returning to Stuttgart very soon. I will make sure you have the very latest on the case by the time you arrive.'

'Thank you for that,' David said. 'I hope I will receive something from you shortly.' David was amazed that he had stumbled on some priceless information from the officer's slip of the tongue. It did however; confirm his worst fears, that the Swiss police and the Mustermanns had been secretly sharing information behind the scenes.

David was not surprised when he received a call from Franz a few days later.

'I trust you are well and managing to put the memory of Anna's disappearance behind you,' Franz said.

'It hasn't been easy, but I'm learning to cope,' David replied. 'I think you have called me to ask that I return to Stuttgart and to my job as Director of Finance.'

'Yes! that is exactly what I am calling you about,' said Franz. 'I would like you back by Friday of this week. You have one final assignment to complete. If that goes well, you will be released from your contract and be free to leave the Mustermann Corporation, and do whatever you like.'

'I understood this was the deal. You explained this to me some time ago. I will plan to travel to Stuttgart on Thursday, arriving in the evening,' David said.

'I will look forward to seeing you then,' said Franz, as he put down his phone.

David packed quickly. He was working on the assumption that Anna wouldn't be coming back. Once he had completed his assignment, he would leave Germany and get back to England as soon as possible. He only needed to pack clothes for a few days. A small case and a shoulder bag would do. He planned to leave in the morning, as soon as he had completed his memory test.

As he drove through Penshurst, he had an uneasy feeling deep down inside. He told himself it was because this was the end of another chapter in his life, albeit a brief one. He was stepping into the unknown. In the past, he had always got another job to go to before he left the previous one. This time it was different and in some ways more exciting, to be stepping out into the unknown. David encouraged himself with the thought that in a few days he would be free from the shackles of the Mustermann Empire. Free to pursue whatever was on offer back in the UK. This is what excited him to drive across Europe and into Germany.

David parked his car in the centre of Stuttgart, removed his two bags and walked in the direction of the flat. As he approached the block of flats, he noticed a light shining from the window of the flat he had shared with Anna. He stopped to check. It was definitely their flat. He must have forgotten to switch it off in his hurry to get away from Stuttgart all those weeks ago. He took the lift to the fourth floor and then fumbled to find his key. The door wasn't locked and as he stepped inside, he was completely unprepared for what he saw. Across the room stood Anna looking dishevelled and agitated. David dropped what he was carrying and made straight for her, intending to catch her up in his arms. But Anna held up her arms to keep him away.

'No! I can't,' she cried.

'How did you get here?' David asked.

'A friend gave me a lift.'

'Does he happen to drive a blue Subaru by any chance?'

'You guessed, from the incident on the Autobahn!'

'No wonder you couldn't be found in Schilthorn or in Mürren. You'd been taken away.'

'I'm sorry,' said Anna. 'I had no choice.'

'About what?'

'Everything,' she murmured.

'Do you mind if I pour myself a drink?' David asked. 'I have a suspicion this is going to take a long time to sort out.'

'There is no drink,' replied Anna. 'No wine, no beer.'

'Where's it gone?'

'This place has been home for hit men for several weeks. They've used and abused whatever they could get their hands on, including me!'

'What do you mean?'

'I've been raped several times. They're just like animals.'

David was filled with revulsion at the thought of his beautiful Anna being cruelly treated by sexual hooligans. The colour of his cheeks gave away his increasing anger.

'Who are they?' he asked.

'I don't know for sure,' Anna replied. 'The ones here are thugs that are paid to eliminate people to order.'

'Where do Klaus and Franz fit in? Are they on the same side as the hit men, or are they likely to be the next ones to be killed?'

'I've no idea! I've given up trying to make any sense of it all,' said Anna.

David sought to encourage her with memories from the past.

'Do you remember some of the first times we met in Carentan and La Haye-du-Puits in August 2014? You told me you were employed as a nanny by Klaus and Sophia, to look after Franz. You said you lived with the Musterman family in a castle above Stuttgart. When I told this to Emma, she found it difficult to believe this was true. I believed every word you said. Was Emma right or was I right?' he asked.

'Emma was right to doubt some of the stories I told. I could see you were infatuated with me and I realised I could get away with embellishing the truth to suit my purposes!'

'OK! I admit I was smitten with you from the first day we met. As hard as it will be to hear, I want you to tell me the truth.'

Anna looked at the floor as she went on to speak in a faltering voice.

'I was born to ageing parents in Freiburg, Eastern Germany. I had a normal childhood and the one thing I enjoyed was learning languages.'

'So first let's clear up your connection with the Baader-Meinhorf gang,' said David.

'There was no connection. I am not related to any members of the gang in any way,'

'Why did you make up such a complicated story to describe your early life?' asked David.

'The stories about the gang were well known and as time went by more revelations came out. To many young Germans they were cult figures. I began to find out more about the individual members, but I never joined the group or tried to make contact with any of them.'

'So the story about you being transported across Europe and ending up in Sicily was made up.'

'Yes, I'm sorry it was.'

'But why?'

'It was a credible story I made up on the spur of the moment. I saw how it got your attention and had you hanging on my every word.'

'If there was no Sicilian connection, there was no need for you to be brought back to Germany.'

'Exactly!' Anna was enjoying her storytelling role and was becoming more relaxed.

'I must admit the thought of those against the Baader-Meinhorf gang kidnapping you in order to keep you from associating with former gang members did puzzle me,' said David.

'I wonder if I had overdone that bit and it might give me away.'

'What happened when you left school? How did you meet up with the Mustermanns?'

'I went to University,' Anna admitted. I was like most other students. I worked hard and enjoyed the social life and frequent parties. I put myself on the pill at that time and I have been on it for over twenty years.

That's why I could be so certain that I wouldn't get pregnant by having sex with you!'

'I was not the first then?' David asked.

'Far from it,' Anna replied. 'Towards the end of my last year at university I saw a vacancy for a nanny to look after a child due to be born in a matter of weeks. The advert had been placed by Sophia Mustermann. I wasn't too interested in being a nanny, but I had heard about the Mustermann family and the empire it had created. I thought there might be an opportunity to find employment with them after I was no longer needed as a nanny. This is how things worked out. My ability with languages was a great advantage. Klaus saw my potential and appointed me as Company Secretary after a few months. Later I was asked to be Financial Officer. All the training I needed was paid for by the Mustermann Corporation.'

'Was your life with the Mustermanns more or less as you described it?' asked David.

'Yes, but there were aspects of the work you knew nothing about.'

'Such as?' David enquired.

'I would infiltrate various businesses, with a view to the Mustermann Corporation acquiring a foothold and then making a take-over bid in due course. After a short time the business would be shut down, workers would be made redundant and it was later discovered the pension funds had been emptied. In the time you've worked for the Mustermanns, you have experienced some of the bullying tactics they employ.'

'But I thought this came from their lack of experience in financial matters or from a genuine oversight to show courteous consideration.'

'Oh no! This was the way they intended it to be. Remember Klaus and Franz are descendents of Max Mustermann,' said Anna, 'Can't you recall the time when I was looking for a job in London and I laughingly said I would apply for something at International Financial Services. I did actually manage to obtain a post there.'

'Something else you need to clear up for me,' David said. 'You must have friends in very high places to be appointed by the European Union as a Goodwill Ambassador for Children.'

'It was set up by the Mustermanns! The whole thing was a charade; the appointment never existed,' Anna confessed.

'You'll have to explain,' David said.

'I was never chosen by the EU to be a Goodwill Children's Ambassador. Klaus arranged that, including the letters and certificates, but it was a hoax. The refugee crisis came at a convenient time to provide cover for me to be away and learn illegal financial techniques.'

David couldn't believe what he was hearing. 'What happened when you went away on training weekends and when you spent time with refugees?'

'It had nothing to do with refugees. I've never seen a refugee! Training was all to do with fraud and deception. I had to learn techniques to develop relations with all manner of businesses. Very often firms would express gratitude to us for warning them against scams and deception. Little did they know we had used these techniques to gain access to their systems and acquire classified information.'

'This smacks at hypocrisy,' David shouted. 'I was trying to reduce corruption in the day-to-day working of the Musterman Corporation and all the time they were perpetuating it on as grand scale!'

'That's often how things are,' said Anna. 'I was sent on fact-finding missions to London when I was employed by the Mustermanns. I posed as a German lady seeking to gain experience in London's financial institutions, but I was actually finding out top-secret information and relaying it back home. As I told you, I did obtain a post with IFS. The idea was to make it unstable and fit for take-over. Brian was chosen to set the change in motion and devise a scheme to get rid of you. It was a pity you fell in love with someone from the enemy camp! Brian was always going to be disposable. He didn't fit into the long-term plans. When he had done his job, he went. Fortunately he became addicted to the drugs he was peddling and that saved someone the job of eliminating him.'

David was horrified to learn about all that was going on behind the scenes at IFS and the Mustermann Corporation. He had no idea this was happening right under his nose.

'Just to conclude this part of the story,' said Anna. 'If you travel to London and visit the IFS building in a few weeks time, you will find it is now under new ownership, with Mustermann Corporation emblazoned across the exterior of the building.'

'It's strange,' said David, 'I had an inkling that something like that was going to happen!' He remained silent for several minutes. Then he felt he had to ask the Question that had kept popping into his mind throughout this conversation with Anna, 'What does all this mean for the future of our relationship?'

'I can't say,' said Anna. 'I wouldn't have thought you would want any more to do with me, a slut and a liar!'

David looked anxious. 'None of us is perfect,' he said. 'Remember, I still love you.'

At that moment the door opened and two figures in black and wearing masks entered the room. They each carried a pistol and they walked over to where David was sitting. They raised their pistols and gestured for him to stand up. Blood drained from his face and he felt sick in the pit of his stomach. Anna looked distraught. The men pushed David towards the door and followed him out of the room.

A few seconds later the sound of a single shot reverberated around the flat.

Anna sank to her knees.

Moments later Franz poked his head round the door. 'He's dead!' he announced. 'I've done my bit. Now Klaus has to clear up!'

Anna wept bitterly.